GOD ENDER

GOD ENDER

WEREWITCH™ BOOK SIX

RENÉE JAGGÉR

Bailey leaned against a wall beside the bar. Her three younger brothers had taken up the stools. She probably could have squeezed in next to them, but these days, even when relaxing with a beer, it was wise to keep an eye on things. From her current position, she could watch anyone who wandered into the Bristling Elk.

"So," asked Jacob, who was eldest of the three, though still younger than Bailey, "you gonna tell us how Boise was? We still haven't heard the whole story. I mean, now that the secret's out that you and Roland are 'together,' a lot of it is probably romantic shit we don't need to hear, but at least it'd be nice to know what the scenery's like and that kind of thing."

Before the girl could respond, Kurt, the youngest of them, piped up with, "If by 'romantic' you mean 'X-rated,' then yeah, sounds right."

Jacob and Russell, the middle brother, took turns swatting Kurt on the back of the head while Bailey glared at him. She ignored Kurt's remark. Instead, she answered Jacob's original question.

"It was okay. Nice, really. Obviously a lot bigger than Greenhearth, but not as big as Portland or Seattle. It's like a decent-sized city that seems halfway acceptable to someone from a small town, if that makes sense. And it's surrounded by all these rolling brown hills that loom between the buildings. Not as impressive as the Cascades, but...different. I liked it. So did Roland."

Russell shifted on the stool. At six foot seven, he was so large that he could barely position himself on it comfortably. "Heard you got into some trouble in Bend." He clenched and unclenched his massive hands.

Tomi, the usual waitress in the afternoon and evening, strolled by. She spent most of her time in the diner wing, whereas the bar was located front-and-center with its attached dance floor off to the left. Keeping an eye on the bar patrons was also part of her duties, though.

"Well," she interjected, "if Russell was there, I'm sure there was no trouble at all unless he started it." As she said this, she ran a hand briefly along the huge young lycanthrope's shoulder and flashed him a mischievous smile.

He grunted. "I wasn't. Needed to stay here and protect the town."

Tomi laughed. "Must have done something right, since it's been peaceful again. For now." She batted her eyes and disappeared into the kitchen.

Bailey watched the scene with a cool eye. She was used to Tomi and the other waitresses and other women in general flirting with her brothers, particularly Russell and Jacob. Tomi was a good ten years Russell's senior, but she felt it was their choice whether to respond to all the swooning and insinuations.

It occurred to her, though, that women might find them even more attractive these days thanks to their connection to *her*. She'd become a celebrity.

"About Bend," Bailey said. "Yeah, minor scuffle at a nice little redneck bar outside town. Buncha goddamn Californians have moved to that place lately, which made the good old boys especially hostile to out-of-towners, I guess. I managed to fix them up without getting us sent to jail."

Jacob raised his beer in a toast. "Best of both worlds."

The front doors opened just then, and in strode a quartet of people who were themselves out-of-towners in Greenhearth, Oregon. Bailey was getting used to visits from werewolves from all over the Pacific Northwest, but the four newcomers were not Weres.

Three of them were women and one was a man, all in their early twenties, comparable ages to her brothers. They were dressed head to toe in black and had an odd assortment of piercings and dyed hair. It was some kind of punk or goth fashion thing, although Bailey paid too little attention to subcultures to judge the specifics.

They didn't look friendly, either.

"Hey," opened the apparent leader, a wiry girl in a corset with a blue streak in her black hair, "we're looking for Bailey Nordin. Are you her? Or is she here somewhere? We heard she hangs around this place."

The three brothers turned around, slowly and unison.

Bailey smiled with frosty politeness. "That's me. How can I help you ladies and gentleman?"

Blue Streak folded her arms in front of her and tapped

at one forearm with her azure-enameled nails. "We saw that scrying broadcast. Both of them. It's weird how after the Venatori sent out the first one—you know, exposing you—your supposed boyfriend then sent out that other one contradicting it. Where is he, anyway?"

Mimicking the girl's gesture, Bailey straightened up from the wall and made eye contact with the newcomers. "He's resting. He almost died helping us drive the Venatori out of this town, and then I tired him right out when we took a little vacation together. Why, did you want to interview him for a podcast or something?"

By now, Bailey had surmised that her visitors were witches. They weren't agents of the Venatori, at least. The fanatical European cult would have either shot first and asked questions later, or perhaps would have tried to ingratiate themselves first and then stabbed her in the back.

No, the childish standoffishness and pseudo-aggression of the quartet suggested they were nothing more than dumbasses looking for trouble. And they'd probably find it.

"Hmm," Blue Streak pretended to consider, tilting her head and turning her eyes toward the ceiling, "I dunno, we'll have to think about it. I mean, it would be interesting to see how the all-powerful werewitch from this dumpy little hick town managed to defeat one of the strongest witch-forces in recent memory. Are you sure the Venatori didn't just decide you weren't worth the trouble?"

Bailey glowered. "Pretty sure."

Jacob asked, "You got this, Bailey? We're here if you need us."

"Oh, yeah," the werewitch replied, stretching and

setting her beer down on the bar's surface. "I'm fine. Think I can handle one little interview."

"Good," the leader of the newcomers interjected. "Since the other thing we're wondering is if you and the Venatori are working together. Their recruiters keep popping up everywhere in Salem. Portland, too, from what I hear. How do we know they're not paying you to scare us into their arms?"

Bailey gestured toward the dance floor with her chin. "Let me show you."

She led the way to the square wooden space, empty of revelers at this hour, while the bartender shot a wary eye at her. He probably didn't want the cops showing up at his establishment yet again. Bad for business.

Bailey didn't think that a police presence would be necessary, though.

She turned to her new friends. "Don't wreck the place. We already had a brawl a month or so back, not to mention the roof took some fire damage a couple of weeks ago."

Blue Streak, glaring with a skeptical sneer, responded by rearing back and tossing a blazing fireball at Bailey's face. Since the girl had telegraphed her attack in advance, the werewitch was able to easily block it, snuffing out the flames with a shimmering disc-shaped arcane shield.

As the leader hurled her crude blast, two of her minions came at Bailey's flanks. The lone male among them reached her first, swinging his arms toward her face, augmenting his speed through magic.

Bailey left her shield hanging in midair to finish extinguishing the fireball and provide an obstruction to further attacks. Then she flash-stepped backward so the young man overshot his swipe and palm-punched him in the side of the face. It didn't take much force since Weres are stronger than humans or witches, even in human form.

"Ugh!" the guy cried out, his head reeling aside, and he stumbled back, dizzy and with a bleeding lip.

Then the other witch, an overweight girl of maybe eighteen or nineteen, tried to tackle Bailey. The werewitch kicked her straight and hard in the solar plexus, halting her charge and making her double over in breathless nausea.

Blue Streak and the other girl with her were collaborating on a spell they probably thought would be clever or impressive. Bailey just hit them both with a wave of telekinetic force with a little sonic disturbance thrown in, so both were blasted off their feet to land on the wood floor with heads ringing.

Then the werewitch magically grabbed the two casters who'd rushed her, threw them into a heap besides their companions, and summoned a sheet of freezing rain to descend on all four.

"Shit!" Blue Streak cursed. "That's fucking *cold!* And you're ruining my makeup!"

"Whoops," Bailey said in a flat voice. "You wanna keep fighting? I didn't break a sweat yet, so I'm good if you're still feeling feisty."

The quartet all got to their feet as the frigid water stopped falling, wiping their clothes off and checking themselves for injury. It was clear that they *didn't* want to continue their "interview," but the leader refused to surrender.

By now, three local pack-alphas, including Will Waldsbach of the South Cliffs, had drifted into the front drinking area from the dining wing and were looking toward the dance floor. They were alert, with shoulders and legs spread in wide fighting stances. Not alarmed but ready.

Will took in the scene at a glance. "You need any help getting rid of them, Bailey?"

The girl waved a hand. "These kids got loose from detention, I'd guess. Show 'em the door, please and thank you."

The four witches groaned and muttered a few half-assed protests as the alphas grabbed them by their drenched collars, hoisted them up, and escorted them out the front entrance and into the parking lot, giving each a good shove toward the road. The casters wisely kept walking and did not look back.

Bailey nodded to her alphas. "Thanks, guys. You can all go back and finish eating. Think I'm gonna finish my beer."

They chuckled and returned to the diner. The were-witch strolled back to the bar, where Jacob handed her the cold bottle she'd left behind.

The bartender-slash-proprietor gave her an appreciative nod, a subtle smile on his heavy face. "Clean up that water, will ya?"

"Oh, right," Bailey agreed. She turned and snapped her fingers, heating a patch of air where the freezing rain had fallen so that it evaporated, leaving the dance floor nice and dry.

Jacob sipped his beer and looked at his sister. "You've grown up, you know?" he quipped. "Not too long ago, you would've just beat them all to a pulp until the sheriff's deputies showed up for their protection. These days, you've got enough self-control to do the minimum necessary to get rid of them and shut 'em up."

With all the heroic shit she'd done lately, it was becoming commonplace for people to praise her, but she tried to stay appreciative and not let it go to her head.

"Thank you, Jacob, and I mean that. I'm working on it. The more I think about it, the stupider I was until pretty damn recently. Four or five months ago might as well have been half a lifetime, with everything that's changed."

Kurt laughed. "I know, right? To think, there was once a fabled time when our town *didn't* keep having to stop crazed-ass witches from burning everything down."

Russell added his two cents. "At least you're free of the marriage obligation."

Bailey nodded and sipped her beer, looking blithe and a tad sarcastic and saying nothing. For all the terrible things that had happened, Russell had reminded her of one of the good occurrences. Come her twenty-fifth birthday, which was almost upon her, she'd be free. The traditional requirement that a female werewolf be wed to an eligible male was waived in the case of shamans.

The door opened behind them. Sensing a subdued aura of magic, Bailey momentarily wondered if the stupid out-of-towners had returned, but she dismissed the notion at once.

It was Roland. He looked healthier than he had even a week ago. He recovered from injury faster than normal humans seemed to, but he'd been on the brink of death during their last battle, so it had taken time for him to get back to one hundred percent.

He greeted them with his customary air of relaxed

confidence. "Hi. Did you have visitors recently? There's a slight…disturbance in the air, you might say."

Kurt chimed in first. "Yeah, some edgy kid-witches from Salem tried to start shit because they ran out of enough energy drinks to keep playing *Vampire: The Masquerade* or whatever. Bailey persuaded them to get lost without the sheriff needing to show up."

Bailey nodded.

Striding to her side, Roland put an arm around her waist. "She's getting better at that, isn't she? Did anyone order her a second beer yet?"

She planted a quick kiss on his lips. "Nah. One's enough for now. It's only, what, two in the afternoon. In fact, I could use some lunch. What about you, Seattle Boy?"

"Sounds great," the wizard agreed. He looked at her brothers. "Gentlemen?"

Jacob waved a hand. "Spend some quality time with each other. We'll wait and have dinner instead."

"Fair enough." Roland tugged gently on his girlfriend's shirt, and the two of them rounded the corner into the diner wing.

The three alphas and their lieutenants noticed the pair at once and gave them polite nods of acknowledgment, which Bailey returned. She picked out a small table in the rear interior corner, putting them as far away as possible from anyone who might want to bother them.

Tomi, on her next round, noticed that they'd come in to eat and approached to take their order.

Bailey did not bother looking at the menu. "The usual," she said, meaning a steak sandwich. "And coffee for us both."

Roland squinted. "You serve breakfast food all day, right? Good. I'll have the vegetable and cheese omelet."

"No problem." Tomi took the menus away and strode off to send their food order to the kitchen.

Once they were alone, Bailey extended her foot under the table and placed it atop Roland's. "Y'know, we oughta take vacations more often," she observed.

He smiled. "I'll agree to that. Sadly, we're a bit busy these days, but this too shall pass. Then I say we take an even longer road trip to Florida or Maine or something. Or Alaska. Wherever you'd like to go."

She tapped her lips with her fork. "I'll think it over."

They talked of other things, enjoying each other's casual company until their meals arrived. Tomi set the steaming platters in front of them and promised to refill their coffee directly. Once she had, they ate in comfortable silence.

"So," Roland began after a moment, prodding his omelet with a fork to release steam and heat from its interior, "while I've had all this downtime lately, I've been tuning in to the witchy gossip sphere. Paying attention to the chatter that comes down the grapevine, that sort of thing."

Bailey hoisted her sandwich and took a bite. "Oh? Anything juicy?"

"Of course." He picked up his knife and carved off a chunk of egg, forking it into his mouth and chewing with relish. "After the infamous mass-scrying broadcasts from a couple weeks ago, there was, you might say, a general reevaluation of the entire situation. Especially regarding the subject of you."

"Figures," Bailey remarked. "I'm getting kinda tired of being the center of everyone's attention. Anonymity has its advantages."

"Well," Roland went on, "mostly it's *positive* attention, or at least neutral. You came out looking pretty good to the world at large, including the world of wizardry and witchcraft. The Venatori, by contrast, made asses of themselves. Oh, sure, there are a handful of people out there who assume they were telling the pure and honest truth, and that we were the ones who faked the second broadcast as damage control. But for the most part, I'd say the gamble worked out."

The girl nodded. "That's good. Next time, though, I'd prefer it if you didn't gamble with your *life*. If you leave me alone at this point, I'll have to come into the afterlife to kick your ass."

"Aw," the wizard quipped, smiling, "I love you too, babe. Seriously, though, I'd prefer to keep on living for a while, so I will do my best on that front."

"You better." She pointed a finger at his face before returning to her sandwich.

He waved a hand through the air. "Anyway, about that 'neutral' reaction I mentioned. A lot of people are still tense and uncertain. They don't think you're the bad guy, exactly, yet the whole idea of a powerful caster who isn't one of them, who's raising an army of shifters to boot, makes them nervous. It's the standard low-level xenophobia that always arises between different tribes or species. They don't believe the Venatori propaganda, but in their mind, witches are witches and Weres are Weres. That's how it's always been. Those are people who've chosen to be scared on general principles."

Bailey furrowed her brow. "I see. I don't have any interest in storming anyone's house if they're not doing anything to me. But I guess it's understandable, with them seeing how much heavy artillery we're marshaling and wondering if there might be a misfire. Something like that."

"Exactly," Roland confirmed. "Some of them are forming small local coalitions. Not for offense, but for turtling up—barring the doors and hiding until this whole mess blows over. That obviously means we don't have to worry about them aiding the Venatori, but it also means we can't count on their support."

The werewitch took a sip of coffee and contemplated the information.

"Hmm. I wonder if maybe this is an opportunity to reach out. Like, if I have time, talk to those people and convince them that we're not gonna pull an Attila the Hun on them or their communities. That's more what the Venatori are trying to do. And since they think they have the right to dictate how witches behave as well, I'd imagine they'd start an inquisition among their own kind after they wiped out us Weres."

Roland shrugged. "Perhaps, but it could be dangerous. Everyone in the caster community is on edge. Since all this started, there's a sense that lycanthropes were a 'sleeping giant' with way more power than anyone knew or expected. Witches were aware that the werewolf community had its handful of shamans who had magical abilities, but the sense was that Weres were mostly a backwoods people and the shamans kept things quiet, offered guidance and support, and arbitrated in occasional minor disputes. That sort of thing."

That much, Bailey agreed, was true.

"But now," the wizard continued, "we…you…have been fighting an intercontinental war and countering a massive conspiracy, so the whole thing looks to them like it sprang out of nowhere a month or so ago. Most witches feel like they're sitting on a powder keg."

Frowning, Bailey said, "Yeah, makes sense. And they're mostly right."

The Venatori had assembled in the ritual hall within the great mansion, one of two main edifices that sat upon the property they owned in Lyon, France. Their headquarters also included a modern office building, but their new leader preferred the more traditional locale. She'd set up a throne before the altar at the far end of the hall.

Watching her, and waiting for her to speak, former Grandmistress Gregorovia felt a mixture of awe and trepidation. She herself had been the Order's final authority until two weeks ago when their original goddess had manifested in the flesh. She'd been reduced to the role of right-hand woman, high priestess to a living deity. It was galling to have been relieved of her authority.

But it also took some of the responsibility off her shoulders. And with Aradia in charge, she was more optimistic than ever that they would achieve victory.

The goddess' appearance contrasted noticeably with

that of her followers. She appeared to be thirty at most, whereas the senior Venatori were all women past the threshold of middle age since magic took a lifetime to master. She wore her night-black hair in a piled coiffure like an aristocratic lady of an ancient civilization, and black robes flowed from her body in long waves. Gold jewelry shone at her forehead, throat, wrists, and fingers.

"Sisters, daughters," Aradia began, her voice a curious bubbling whisper that was somehow loud enough to echo. "We have had a respite in which to recover from our Order's recent failure. Now we must resume the fight. The time has come to declare *total war* against the upstart wolves. Are you ready?"

Gregorovia nodded within the hood of her dark burgundy robe. "We are, Lady of Witchcraft. We shall trust in your guidance. You have our full confidence, and we are prepared to be led to ultimate triumph."

Behind and around the former Grandmistress, the other members of the senior council, as well as various high-ranking lieutenants and functionaries, echoed her words.

As with her, there were misgivings among a smattering of the witches. Aradia had founded the Venatori Order in times so distant as to be virtually forgotten, yet this was the first time she'd personally manifested in recorded history, save for the vaguest of rumors from the Classical Roman Era. Some members felt that the deity was usurping their self-governance.

Yet under the lax and lukewarm patronage of the Norse goddess Freya, the Order had received no aid to speak of.

And finally, Freya had all but sided with the lycanthropes against her own people.

It could not be tolerated. Gregorovia was willing to abdicate a portion of her authority for the sake of having a patron who supported them.

The echoing whisper continued. "It is well," Aradia pronounced, "for there shall be no more niceties or indecision. No more picking away at isolated settlements in a haphazard effort to gain the popular support of those witches who lack our commitment and conviction. Rather than scheme, we shall use force, wisely and strategically directed."

"Yes, Lady," Gregorovia agreed. Hearing her prior tactics disparaged rankled, especially since she thought they *had* been using a good strategy. Nonetheless, she awaited the deity's commands.

Aradia smiled. She had a cold, placid, alien beauty, and the expression looked subtly unnerving on her face.

"We know who our primary enemies are. Defeating Bailey and eradicating her race must be our chief goals. We shall start with her, then eliminating the rest shall take almost no effort.

"Therefore, pockets of our best witches shall be dispatched to eliminate her most important people. Pack alphas. Elder shamans. Trusted lieutenants, mentors, and capable agents of every sort. Local and regional allies in the Pacific Northwest of America. We shall kill those whom Bailey Nordin relies upon, leaving her alone, powerless, and ripe for destruction."

The former Grandmistress bowed her head. "It shall be as you wish."

"I," the goddess continued, "will aid you indirectly by appearing before those communities of witches who might be willing to join you, but are afraid to act. With my blessing, we can expect that your ranks will once again swell with volunteers."

Gregorovia closed her eyes. If Aradia's plan worked, it would undo all the damage that traitor Roland had done to their cause in the eyes of other casters.

Aradia's face grew grimmer and frostier. "Because of the universal prohibition on direct intervention by divine beings, I cannot force our brethren to aid you, but I can persuade them to consider it. And many of them will because they know, as we do that the time has come for war. The wolves shall not defeat us!"

CHAPTER TWO

Things remained quiet as day faded into evening. Bailey, Roland, and her brothers walked home. It wasn't too far, and they felt like they could use the exercise and fresh air. Summer had almost arrived, and the weather was warm and pleasant. Vacationers from Portland and Salem drove by on the highway occasionally, and the townspeople waved to them.

It made it easier to ignore all the damage done to buildings in the central square, which might take months to repair.

"Man," Jacob commented, "I just hope it doesn't get much warmer. Here in the mountains, at least we don't get it as bad as the folks down lower on either side of us. Hot and humid to the west, and drier but even hotter to the east. Still, I'll take winter over summer."

Kurt scoffed. "Hah! Easy for you to say. We live in the Pacific Northwest. We don't *have* winter, not really. Unless you go way up high into the snowcaps and shit."

"That would be fine with me." Jacob shrugged. "We're

furry animals in human form, better adapted to cold than heat. If the town gets burned down, I say we pull up stakes and head for Alaska."

Russell made a grunting noise in his throat. "I like the thought of Alaska, but I'm staying and fighting."

Bailey jumped in, trying to stop the conversation from getting too serious. "Yeah, yeah, the snow is always whiter on the other side. Unlike you dipshits, I *have* traveled, and people complain about the weather everywhere. If we make contact with some other species from Alpha Centauri, that's probably the first thing they'll discuss with us."

"Shit," Kurt marveled, "that's one of the deepest things she's ever said! Roland must be rubbing off on her."

The wizard, who'd been following them in bemused silence, quipped, "I try to rub her whenever I can, it's true."

Bailey and Russell both shot him thunderous glances, and he raised his hands in an innocent expression of surprise. "What?"

Soon they were back at the Nordin residence, a century-old farmhouse near the northwestern corner of town. A pole barn out back had become Roland's new quarters. Beyond that, the backyard led to a pine-forested slope.

The grass and trees were still recovering from the magical damage the Venatori had wrought when they'd attacked the werewitch in her home as she slept. They all tried to ignore it.

The Nordin boys threw some chicken and potatoes into the oven and turned on a football rerun from the previous autumn.

Bailey and Roland shared a chair in the far corner of the living room, huddled close together. They didn't say much. It was nice to simply be together and for things to be peaceful.

The girl wondered, though, how her brothers felt about her relationship with the wizard, now that everyone knew about it.

I already pissed a lot of people off by resisting getting married to a Were, she mused, *and here I am dating a male witch. At least almost everyone seems to like him.*

Footsteps approached the house, and everyone except Roland perked up. Then a knock sounded on the door. Jacob got up to answer it.

"Oh, hi, Gunney," he said. The other four relaxed. "Did you want to talk to Bailey?"

"Yeah, if she's not busy."

The werewitch slid off the chair, kissed Roland on the cheek, and marched to the door. "Well, what brings you here? You haven't been to our house in, shit, five or six years."

The aging mechanic was still wearing his smudged overalls, but he'd taken off his baseball cap and held it by his side, so his shaggy hair spilled over his craggy, bearded face.

"True," he conceded, "but better late than never. Listen, I know you could use some time to relax these days, but I got an interesting project up at the shop and wouldn't mind some help."

Bailey smiled. "Sure. Besides, working on cars is relaxing. Just give me a minute here."

She went to the bathroom, said her goodbyes, and

followed Gunney outside to hop into his truck. He drove them the short distance to the auto shop, explaining the gist of the job as the vehicle rumbled down the street.

"It's this old Model T hotrod. Admittedly, it's a kit car, not an original, but you know, still kinda nice. Right now, it's all matte black, but it's the guts that need work first before we worry about the skin."

Bailey chuckled. "No shit. I still need to get *my* car painted, but it's in sound working order, and that's what matters most."

"Indeed."

The old man fell silent for a minute or two, then added, "I need something constructive to do. Business has fallen off. The fucked-up stuff going on means fewer people are out off-roading or taking trips since they don't want to be caught alone in the middle of nowhere, and you know how bored I get when I don't have cars to work on. Not to mention, well, who knows what you'll get up to next, or where you'll go. You've been spending so much time in parallel dimensions—I heard most of the details from Will, by the way—and then you went off to Idaho right when things were calming down again. I'd like us to spend time together while we can."

Unspoken but obvious was the implication that either or both of them might not *have* another chance if the Venatori came back in force. Bailey was like the daughter the older man had never had, and in turn, she'd thought of him as a second father.

They pulled into the parking lot, opened the shop, and wheeled in the Model T.

Gunney summarized the project in more detail. "We've

got a fairly simple assembly here. Gotta put the top of the engine together, though most of it's already under the hood. Still, might take a bit of time. Tell me when you want to call it a night. Oh, and clock in over there so I can pay your ass."

Bailey was way ahead of him. "Yeah, yeah," she called from the time clock.

They set to work at a steady pace, moving purposefully but in no great hurry. The hours whiled away into night as the pair assembled the upper end, the cylinders, and the intake, getting a satisfying coating of grease and grime on themselves and watching as the engine slowly progressed toward viability.

"You ever been to Boise?" Bailey asked. "It's not a place people usually think of to go for a vacation, which I suppose is why Roland and I chose it. We'll do Reno next time, or go down to California if we're feeling adventurous. Hope the smog doesn't kill me."

Gunney laughed. "I've been all over the West. Did a lot of driving around when I was your age or so. Got into some trouble in Boise, though nothing too serious, and the town's probably grown so much since then that I wouldn't recognize the place. I'll tell you the story in exchange for..."

He'd been about to ask Bailey to hand him a rag to wipe off his hands, but she'd extended one toward him before the words had left his mouth.

Madame Bertolio adjusted her shirt. It looked silly in her estimation, and it was uncomfortably tight, but glamor magic would only get them so far. They also had to dress the part. Wearing the traditional Venatori leather uniform in the United States was no longer advisable.

She glanced at her subordinates. "Positions. I will dispatch the signal through the coven-mind when the time is right."

The other eight witches agreed without speaking and surrendered part of their individual wills as Bertolio wove the threads of the coven's mutual consciousness into a tight pattern. Even when physically separated, their thoughts would be well-coordinated.

Two of the sorceresses placed themselves in strategic but inconspicuous places near both the front and rear exits of the nightclub. It was located in a rather dark and labyrinthine part of Seattle, away from the prying eyes of the general public. Most of its clientele wasn't human, after all.

Madame Bertolio flicked her hand, and the seven, including her, moved toward the main doors.

She was young enough that the glamor spell to make her look like an extremely attractive post-college girl did not require massive or obvious outpourings of magic. The women with her were all in their middle or later twenties. They had no problems getting past the bouncer's screening process.

Within, the club was decorated in a faintly neo-gothic style, and shades of purple, green, and deep blue predominated where lighting was concerned. The DJ played a mixture of EBM, metal, darkwave, and industrial, most of it recent, but a sampling of hoary old classics from the '80s and '90s as well.

Bertolio and her posse pretended to engage in idle chatter as they scoped the place out. Anyone who saw them would have assumed they were a gaggle of European students on vacation. Four or five of the male patrons were already eyeing them.

It took little more than a minute and a half for the coven-mind to collectively identify which of the attendees were wolf-shifters. Twelve total, divided evenly between men and women. They were most interested in one of the males, but the witches intended to deal with all of them.

Rather than spread out for a simultaneous multipronged strike, the seven stayed together and chose their positions based on what would make for the fastest straight line through the writhing mass of bodies on the dance floor, as well as some of the more inert ones clustered around the tables and benches along the sides.

A few stupid men approached them and tried to flirt. Bertolio and her subordinates offhandedly replied with vacuous comments, saying just enough to avoid attracting suspicion while also keeping their would-be seducers at arm's length.

The muscular werewolf called Jim, lieutenant to the alpha of the Silver Star pack of southern Washington, had drifted to the far side of the dance floor along with a female Were who seemed to be enjoying his attention. His little vacation in Seattle was going well.

Until now.

Do it, Madame Bertolio thought, and the words spread throughout the coven-mind without audible speech being necessary.

The two witches outside deployed powerful magical

shields that sealed the front entrance and rear fire exit. Out front, the bouncer, gawking in shock, was trapped in the shield and hung like a statue within its viscous arcane field.

Then the seven within the club made their move.

One of the younger witches grabbed the young woman next to them around the neck, pulling her off-balance and into a headlock as Bertolio conjured a sword blade of glowing magenta plasma and plunged it into the were-girl's heart. Her scream rose above the pounding music, then other screams joined and mingled with it.

The witches shoved their way through the crowd, which melted away as panicked revelers flattened themselves against the walls or fled in vain toward the exit.

Bertolio saw a young local witch recording the spectacle with her phone. *Good,* she thought, and broadcast it among the coven. That way, none of her followers would try to aggressively stop the girl from taking video footage.

A final cluster of panicking forms scrambled away, then Jim stood before them alone. He'd tried the rear exit and found it blocked. He had a barstool in his hands, and given his size and strength, it might have been intimidating to a mere human.

"You!" he growled. "When are you bitches going to give it up? We don't want any trouble from you. *Fuck off!*"

He swung the stool. Madame Bertolio threw a lance of concentrated heat and electricity that sheared through it, scattering burnt wood and melting steel in a shower of fragments. Then the lance pierced his torso.

More people screamed.

It is done, Bertolio said to her coven. *Prepare to move out.*

The rear guard dismissed the shield with which she'd

held the door shut and the seven went out the back. The front and rear guards joined them and they wove a cloaking spell over themselves, then separated to run, fly, or hide as needed, giving the authorities too many targets to track at once. They would be out of Seattle before the police or even the Agency knew what had happened.

Before she left, Bertolio sent a small psionic urge back into the club—a magically empowered suggestion that anyone who witnessed tonight's spectacle feel free to talk about it loudly with anyone who would listen.

To send the message that it was open season on shifters.

The Agency had one major regional office for each of the four main Census Bureau designations of the United States. The one that oversaw the West was located in Reno, Nevada, a location deemed reasonably convenient for dispatching agents to any part of an extremely large land area, whether in California, the Southwest, the Rockies, or the Pacific Northwest.

Of course, most of Agent Townsend's business lately had been in the PNW. He'd submitted a request to move their headquarters to Portland or Seattle. He strongly doubted it would happen, but asking made him feel better.

"Goddammit," he muttered under his breath as he strode through the halls. Junior agents and various support personnel, recognizing the sour look on his nondescript face and the purpose in his gait, moved aside to let him through.

He'd been having breakfast in the cafeteria when the

report came in. He could have viewed it on his phone, but the picture was too small, and their reception was garbage anyway. He'd headed back to watch the video on a proper screen.

Unlocking the door with his keycard, he stepped into his office and shut the door behind him. His dinosaur of a computer was still spitting out reams of paper filled with tedious numerical analyses of probable scenarios, correlational data, and other such stuff that he was required to process in order to fill out the metric tons of paperwork the higher-ups demanded.

There was also his laptop. He opened it, brought it to life, and went at once to his inbox.

The email consisted mainly of restating what he'd heard and adding detail. A group of witches had stormed a paranormal-friendly nightclub in Seattle and systematically murdered all twelve of the lycanthropes who'd been present. Then they'd vanished into oblivion. Their identities were unknown.

Townsend snorted. "Unknown. That's downright fatuous, even by HQ standards. Who the fuck else would it be if not our friends from Lyon?"

He opened the attached video link. One of the spectators had recorded the whole incident on their phone and posted the wretched thing to a private forum frequented by members of the supernatural community, especially casters.

The picture was dark, and the person who'd recorded it did not have a steady hand, but the essentials were clear enough. It showed a group of seven women killing their way through a panicking crowd using short-range plasma blades, which were the preferred homicide instruments of the Venatori. They were not as attention-grabbing or hard to control as big, scary projectiles. They could also be conjured out of thin air, meaning the witches didn't need to carry around weapons.

There was one problem, though. The killers were dressed in normal civilian clothes.

"Ugh," Townsend groaned. "Either they finally wised up and stopped wearing those distinctive leather getups, or we're dealing with their patsies. Or possibly copycats, which would amount to the same thing as patsies. Shit. Haven't they learned their lesson by now?"

If it was the Venatori, then they had obviously not since what the video depicted was their most brazen attack yet. It was on a far smaller scale than their two assaults on Greenhearth, yet in those cases, they'd been dealing with a small, isolated town that was used to keeping its secrets from the outside world.

A nightclub in Seattle was different. There would be almost no way to contain the damage or stop the rumors from spreading.

He could contact Bailey Nordin and let her deal with it. She, under the guidance of her shamans, was setting herself up as the savior and leader of American Weres. Yet for that same reason, involving her would necessarily involve the entire shifter community of the Northwest. It'd be another step toward all-out war between shifters and casters.

Normal people, civilians unaware of the supernatural, would be roped in. Some would get hurt or killed, which was what the Agency least wanted to happen.

"So." He sighed, feeling alone and overburdened, "Looks like it's up to us again. Scratch that—up to *me*. I get to step in and mitigate this crap from the front lines, so that by the time it does reach Bailey, it's been halfway resolved. Fuck."

The Nordin girl was the last resort, the insurance policy. What the Agency couldn't deal with today, she and her friends could tomorrow.

But it would be better if it never came to that. Bailey was like a goddamn Horseman of the Apocalypse. The new fifth one, the Horseman of Cover-Up Paperwork and Bureaucratic Fuckery.

Townsend removed his dark glasses and rubbed his eyes. "Spall," he breathed, "you got out at a good time. Enjoy your vacation in heaven. Or hell even, which is probably still better than half the horseshit the Venatori have in mind. Feel free to come back and lend a hand any time, though."

With that, the agent rose to his feet, left his office, and headed for the armory, pausing only briefly to send a text that would be relayed to the other field operatives in the building. A response team was already being put together, so seizing command of them would be a simple matter.

He arrived at the arsenal to find four other agents equipping themselves. He gave them a grunt and a tilt of the head.

"I'll wait," he said, "'til everyone's here before we move on to briefing. Suffice it to say this is not a PR errand or an open battle. It's a *hunt*."

The other men acknowledged his words with solemn nods.

Townsend stripped down to his underclothes and

grabbed a protective vest. It looked much like medieval scale armor, which in turn resembled the body of a fish with its many rounded interlocking plates. It was silver, although the material had an iridescent sheen that resembled no metal known to the average person.

He put his suit back on over the armor and then combed through the available weapons, passing over the larger arcanoplasm rifles in favor of handguns that were weaker but easier to conceal and control. There was another prototype sidearm he might bring, but he'd have to check with the boys in Research & Development first.

He chuckled as he holstered an arcane pistol. "At least this means the Nordin girl will get a little extra time to live a normal civilian life. Temporarily."

CHAPTER THREE

Bailey sighed. "It seems like a shame, getting to drive this thing but only using it to go thirty-fucking-five through the middle of town and so forth. Still, far be it from me to risk Gunney's baby on the freeway again."

Roland concurred. "And you *are* getting to drive it again, in general. That's better than nothing, right?"

Before them, gleaming in the sun, was the mechanic's personal crown jewel, a '79 Trans Am painted and outfitted exactly like the one in Smokey and the Bandit. They'd taken it to Seattle weeks ago and barely managed to keep it from being damaged then. Bailey was pretty sure she could replicate the feat while simply taking it out for a few late-morning errands. She'd walked to work, so Gunney was letting her use the car for the errands.

They climbed in, and Bailey fired up the engine. "If I have to go thirty-five, I'll drive it in style."

"That's the spirit." Roland wasn't much of a car person, but he appreciated the vehicle's distinctiveness and beauty, not to mention the cultural pedigree it carried in certain corners of America.

They drove down to Main Street and cruised along it, drinking in the appreciative looks they got from passing townsfolk. Their destination was the hardware store, where Bailey picked up some toilet bowl cleaner and a box of nails as per her brother's request. Then they headed to one of the side streets near the west rim of the valley. As long as they had the wheels, Bailey figured, it made sense to do a quick security patrol of the town.

Clusters of Weres recognized them and waved or nodded. In addition to the town's own, an honor guard of wolves from other packs and locales rotated in and out of Greenhearth, helping keep an eye on things in the event of another witch attack.

"Well," Bailey commented, "seems like things are okay. I wonder if–"

Roland's phone went off. He pulled it from his pocket and swiped the screen to view the incoming text. He didn't get many messages these days.

His brow furrowed as he gazed at the screen. "What the hell?"

Bailey disliked the undertone of fear in his voice. He tapped something, and a video or audio file started playing —noise, chaos, and screams. "What is it?" she asked.

He waved a hand. "Pull over, please. I need to watch this again and focus on it. It's the kind of thing where it's better to form your own opinion based on what you see, rather than jumping to the same conclusions as the person who sent it."

Now she was worried. She moved the Trans Am off the

road, carefully parking it on a grassy shoulder near a low cliff. Then she leaned over to watch as Roland replayed the video.

It was shaky, and dark aside from flashes of colored light, but the essence was clear. A group of witches was storming through a nightclub or rave or party, killing people as they went. Two or three of the victims looked familiar. And at the end...

"Holy shit, it's Jim. Roger's lieutenant from the Silver Stars. He was with us during the temple trials. And I think one of those women who got killed was the girlfriend of another pack alpha in Washington who showed up to pledge loyalty."

Roland frowned. "That's what I was afraid of. The perpetrators are wearing normal clothes, but their method seems awfully familiar."

Bailey put her hands to her face, suddenly feeling as though the accumulated tiredness of months was weighing down on her despite how well she'd slept last night. "Not this shit again. What's the *matter* with them? Didn't they get the message that we don't want anything to do with them? Didn't we kick their asses hard enough last time?"

The wizard put his phone away. "It was a club in Seattle. I know the place, and I've been there a few times. I wonder if we should go up and check on things, but it might be a trap. Makes me wonder if they're going to move against my family. Then again, they lost a lot of support last time for attacking a fellow witch, so unless they're even stupider than we thought, I doubt it."

Inhaling deeply, Bailey put her hands on the wheel and stared straight ahead. "Instead of checking on things, I'd rather go up there and pound their heads into the pavement. But I'm the shaman of Greenhearth. If they trap us up there or even distract us for a while, we'd be abandoning this town. Shit."

"Good point," Roland acceded. "You're not the shaman of the entire world. Not yet, anyway. I'd be shocked if this *wasn't* partly an attempt to draw you into another conflict, but your first responsibility is to your home town and pack."

The werewitch sat silent, turning it over in her mind. Before she could reach a decision, a hand knocked on the driver's side window.

"*Goddamn, what the fuck?*" she sputtered, practically jumping out of her seat. Roland, too, was waving his hands and swearing. There was no reason why anyone should have been able to sneak up on them so easily.

It was Fenris. "I'm sorry," he rumbled. "I was in a hurry."

Bailey's mentor and teacher, the god of all Weres, was in his usual human form: a tall, broad-shouldered man in his late forties, stubble-jawed and dressed in a bulky hooded coat. He'd called himself Marcus before he'd revealed his true identity. He motioned for them to step outside.

They obeyed. For an instant, the girl wondered if it might have been a Venatori agent disguised as Fenris, but she couldn't detect the kind of magic such a ruse would require. There was only the typical oceanic concentration of power that followed the deity wherever he went.

"I have bad news," Fenris reported. "I was able to discern your location easily and did not want to waste time, so I stepped through a portal straight to this spot. I apologize for startling you at a time when tensions are high."

"It happens." Roland shrugged. "And I'm pretty sure we just heard the news ourselves if you're talking about the nightclub attack in my hometown."

The tall man nodded. "Yes. And two other pack alphas in Washington have died under mysterious circumstances. It would seem the Venatori have moved on to the next phase in their plan."

Bailey looked aside in a futile effort to hide her grief and rage. "Goddammit. I'm so tired of people dying for no good reason. When is there gonna be an end to this crap? Roland and I were discussing whether we should head up to Seattle to help, but well, my duties as shaman start in Greenhearth."

Fenris took a step toward her and laid a hand on her shoulder. "That is correct. It's good to help all our people whenever and wherever you can, but first you must see to your own community. Whatever the Venatori are up to, there's certainly more to come, and this town might once again be in the crosshairs. I would expect their next move sooner rather than later. You are not responsible for every single life in North America, and Greenhearth needs you after all it's been through lately."

Roland begrudgingly folded down the passenger's side seat of the Trans Am and allowed Fenris to slip into the back. "For such a nice car," the wizard remarked, "you'd think they could have splurged on four doors rather than two."

Ignoring him, Fenris told them to drive back into town. "We should hole up somewhere defensible. Probably not your home, so we don't endanger your family again. I will need time to look into the current matter and see what I can discern."

"Okay," Bailey agreed. "I know exactly the place."

Agent Townsend paused his team for a quick review before they stormed the basement. The place had originally been a packing plant in the industrial area of Tacoma, but these days, it was mostly rented out for raves. Especially the kind frequented by supernatural folk.

"Okay," said Townsend, "everyone needs to remember the directive. We start using nonlethal hand-to-hand restraint techniques since we want prisoners rather than corpses. If they resist, which they probably will, we use the knives. Arcanoplasm pistols are a last resort. Clear?"

"Yes, sir," the other agents replied.

Townsend gave them a short demonstration of how the prototype knives worked. He drew his own from its sheath. In profile, it was of a fairly typical military style, a drop-point blade about eight inches in length. The metal gleamed brighter than steel, however. It looked like chrome or even pearl.

When the agent flicked it, it gave off a slight spark and seemed to be humming on an infrasonic level.

"These things," he explained, "are charged with an arcano-electric current that will pass into the body of a witch at the slightest cut or puncture. It gets into their bloodstream and interferes with their biochemistry in a way that's been shown to inhibit the use of magic. I don't understand the nitty-gritty of it, but it's proven effective in tests. Use the knives to wound or incapacitate if possible, but you are authorized to kill if necessary."

With that, the squad, consisting of nine men and one woman, marched down the stairs to the basement, where lights flashed and music throbbed. There was only the one exit, in flagrant violation of the local fire code, and a handful of anti-magic devices had been hidden in the surrounding streets and lots to prevent any of the sorceresses from trying to teleport out of the immediate area. There remained the risk, though, that some of them might escape via longer-distance teleportation.

The agents were dressed in formal yet unofficial clothes and were not wearing their usual distinctive dark glasses. This was a different kind of mission, and it demanded a different approach, especially with the Venatori having made the shift to disguising their own presence.

The doorman waffled about letting them in, but he relented once Townsend slipped him a pair of twenty-dollar bills. The ten men stepped into the rave.

No one paid them any heed, aside from half a dozen or so near the entrance who spared them a single glance and then returned to their intoxicated revelries. Everyone was dancing in an ecstatic stupor, fixated on seducing one another or massively tripping on drugs. Townsend and his men could have crashed the party in full uniform and most of the clientele would not have cared or noticed.

It was a diverse crowd. Witches and wizards, certainly. Most were unaffiliated locals.

A smattering of vampires. By now, Townsend had learned to pick them out, and they were more common than usual in sunlight-deprived Seattle and its satellite cities. They had a noticeable pallor, even the ones from darker-skinned ethnic backgrounds, and moved in a quick, slightly unnatural way that reminded the agent of a lizard or a snake.

Speaking of reptiles, there were also a few ophidian face-changers. Such people were rare, and fortunately for the Agency, they could only disguise themselves with a single human visage that was modeled on their true, serpentine features. It gave them an odd and distinctive look.

He wasn't sure about lycanthropes, though. Two or three big, hairy men presented likely candidates, but more investigation would be required.

Furthermore, it was possible that the witch cult's little affair yesterday had convinced the entire shifter population to stay home and lie low for a while.

Townsend dispatched his troops to different parts of the dance floor through the use of hand signals. Identifying the undercover Venatori would require effort, but not much time. He expected the mission to be over within ten minutes, tops.

Four minutes passed before one of his subordinates, Agent Velasquez, spoke into his earpiece. "Six lovely ladies in the northeast corner. I think laying the moves on them could result in a very productive night, my man."

"Roger," Townsend replied, his voice scarcely audible under the pulsating electronic music.

He and the others closed in on Velasquez's position and spotted their targets. Half a dozen women—three of whom looked a little old to be attending a rave, but then again,

Townsend was well into middle age himself—were standing in a cluster and talking among themselves. Taken out of context, they would not have been suspicious.

But their clothing and faux-casual demeanor and glamor spells could not disguise the fact that they did not blend in. Something about them was...*off.*

The witches noticed the team at the moment all ten of them were assembled.

"Now," Townsend barked.

The agents pounced, grappling with the four ladies out in front while the remaining two hung back and raised their hands to cast spells. If they decided to cut loose, casualties would be significant. But Townsend was counting on them having orders to avoid collateral damage, given the Venatori's recent PR debacle at Greenhearth.

The four witches who'd been seized shouted protests in English, French, and Italian, trying to keep up the charade that they were ordinary partygoers on holiday from Europe. But the two in the rear were panicking. One conjured a plasma sword, and the other formed a crackling fireball in the palm of her hand.

Townsend tussled with a petite French woman. Despite her size, she'd used magic to subtly augment her strength, and he was having trouble subduing her. He noticed the two deadly spells about to be cast.

"Knife 'em!" he shouted.

One agent hurled his blade, the spinning weapon grazing the shoulder of the witch with the fireball, while another lunged and stabbed the one with the plasma sword in the thigh. Both women shrieked and stumbled back into the wall, their bodies shuddering from the infusion of arcano-electric current. Their spells died in their hands.

Then the true fanatical desperation of the Venatori was made manifest. The witch struggling with the lone female agent next to Townsend detonated an explosion centered on herself.

The world cracked asunder, and Townsend's vision went black as the concussion and heat and sonic force drove him head over feet through the air. Faintly he saw the stampede of the terrified crowd as they tried to get away from the blast. Most of them fled toward the sole exit, although a few just pressed themselves against the far walls. Concrete, metal, and plaster cracked and smoked.

Townsend crashed to the floor. Most of his body was numb, and he could barely see or think. His ears rang and throbbed; he couldn't hear anything else. Struggling not to pass out, he lifted his head and looked toward the scene of the brawl.

Three of the witches and five of the agents were dead, or almost dead, and one or two bystanders also lay still upon the ground. Fires burned here and there. Townsend's men were still too disoriented to act.

The surviving sorceresses tossed lightning into the wires and rafters, sending a barrage of sparks through the basement and shorting out most of the electrical equipment. The music ceased and the normal lights winked out, leaving only a pair of dim emergency lamps embedded in the walls. In the resulting confusion, the witches fled through the crowd and vanished up the stairs.

Townsend looked down at himself. One of his arms and most of his body below the navel were severely burned.

"Oh, fuck," he rasped. "This is…the apotheosis…of fuckery. I'm…fucked." He coughed up blood.

Agent Velasquez ran to his side and shouted something. It looked like "Sir!" followed by his name, but all the senior agent could hear was the persistent muffled ringing.

His vision was starting to fade. *At least,* he thought, *we picked off another handful of them and stopped them from killing any shifters here. That means other Weres won't retaliate against innocent witches and kick off a total shitstorm. I'd say this mission almost qualifies as a success. At worst, it was a stalemate.*

"Spall," he croaked, unable to perceive his own voice, "looks like…we finally–"

Everything went black.

***

"Damn, I'm hungry," Gunney grumbled. "It's impressive that the sandwich shop stayed in business after the damage they took in that battle the other week, but I woulda thought the cheesesteaks would be here by now. Probably should have just gone and picked them up."

Bailey sipped orange soda from a glass bottle. "At least we have plenty to drink in the meantime."

"Yeah," the mechanic acknowledged. "Dunno why, but I had a feeling we might all be getting thirsty soon, though I'd like something a little stronger. How did you guys come to the conclusion that my shop was the best place to wait for a goddamn siege, anyhow? I'm happy to help, but I'd rather not lose my business."

Roland raised a finger. "Well, you *did* weather a siege last time the Venatori attacked, didn't you?"

Gunney frowned. "True."

They all languished on shop stools behind the main auto bays, trying to enjoy the pleasant weather despite the awkward circumstances. Bailey and Roland had spent the night in the office, and while Gunney trusted them, it wasn't something he was used to.

The Nordin brothers were worried, too. Bailey had told them the truth—that they had reason to believe the Venatori might try something, but so far, there was no clear threat. Until further notice, she'd rather not put her home in danger.

"Okay," Jacob had said over the phone, "but we're gonna come by and check on you later, and give us a call every couple hours, okay?"

She'd agreed.

Gunney finished his soda and tossed the bottle into a plastic-lined bin. "Those goddamn scum-sucking bitches," he muttered. "Pardon my French, but shit. They got us fortifying our homes and businesses and jumping at shadows because of this crap they pulled two hundred miles away in Seattle. They're like the guy who loses an argument, so he runs away spewing petty-ass insults and then comes back and slashes your tires two nights later. I ain't never gonna trust a witch again after this."

Roland cleared his throat, and the mechanic looked at him.

"Present company excluded, of course. Substitute 'Venatori' for 'all witches,' though it's disturbing how many of the regular ones sided with them. At first, anyhow."

Bailey cracked her neck. "We changed a lot of their minds. Fenris, what do you make of this? Any insights?"

The towering shaman crouched in a shadowed corner of the shop's exterior, sitting comfortably on dust and gravel. "I am confused," he admitted. "Even for zealots, their actions make no sense. After their crushing defeat, they should have backed off. Either given up altogether, or at least spent a month, three months, or even six recuperating and reconsidering. Yet they're pressing on with more strikes against Weres only two weeks later. Why? What is spurring them on?"

Footsteps approached, and someone offered an answer to Fenris' rhetorical question.

"A god," the voice stated. "Well, a goddess."

Everyone looked up. The newcomer was a lean, athletic Latino man in his early to mid-thirties with sleek black hair and a deep bronze tan. They'd never seen him before, but his attire made him instantly recognizable—a suit of dark gray-green, not quite black, coupled with sunglasses.

Bailey did a quick magical scan on the guy to ensure he wasn't a witch in disguise. He checked out, and therefore must be a legitimate messenger of the Agency.

"Hi," she greeted him. "I'll assume you know who we are. Who are you, and where's Townsend? He busy?"

The young agent frowned, and when he replied, it was obvious that he was choking back on something painful. His tone of voice made Bailey's gut clench before his words registered in her mind.

"Agent Townsend was severely hurt last night during an operation in Tacoma," he stated. "One of the Venatori we were tracking suicide-bombed herself, and Townsend and four other agents were near her. Three died, and another man of ours is alive but in critical condition. I was there and didn't escape entirely unscathed, either."

Bailey noticed that there was bulk that might indicate bandages on his chest and shoulder under his suit and around his right wrist.

"Jesus," Gunney lamented, putting a hand to the bridge of his nose.

"I..." Bailey started. "I'm sorry. I'm not sure what to say. Townsend is one of our strongest allies. He's helped me a lot. Is there something we can do to help?"

She hadn't known him well on a personal basis, but it still stung her terribly. She was getting sick of having friends hurt or killed.

The agent shook his head to clear it and focus rather than in response to anything the girl had said. "Townsend acted bravely, and we stopped them from killing any more Weres for the time being. I'm Agent Velasquez. Townsend appointed me to be your new contact with the Agency in the event that anything happened to him."

Bailey nodded. "Nice to meet you, Velasquez, although I wish it could've been under happier circumstances. We heard about the attack in Seattle two nights back. Thought about coming to help, but we figured the Venatori were setting a trap to draw us away from Greenhearth."

"Yes," he acknowledged, affecting the blunt and stoic demeanor of a federal operative to the best of his ability. "That had occurred to us, as well. But there's been an even more important development, and we wanted you to stay in the loop, given your importance to the overall situation."

A car pulled up on the other side of the repair bays, and out stepped the sandwich shop's delivery girl.

"Well," Roland said, "pull up a stool, and you can have half my cheesesteak if you want."

Velasquez passed on the offer of food, but nevertheless sat down and told them the whole story once they were alone again.

"Recently," he began, "we managed to turn one of the prisoners we took from the Venatori. Extracting even a small amount of useful information from them has proven highly difficult, due to their fanaticism and the magical techniques they have to resist interrogation and manipulation. There were some calls to resort to grossly unconstitutional methods, but that sort of thing tends to be unreliable anyway."

"Ugh," Roland remarked. "Well, good for you."

The agent went on, "We used a mixture of threats and promises of clemency, combined with a clever 'shock collar' approach to convince one of them to act as a double agent. We implanted a microexplosive in her via a new experimental surgical procedure, and she had no way of knowing where the device was. A remote signal can be bounced off satellites from entire continents away, at which point it would detonate—not killing her outright, but flooding her bloodstream with a metal particulate we've developed that would slowly poison her and remove her ability to use magic."

Roland raised an eyebrow at that, clearly disturbed by the implication for his species.

"We've also," Velasquez continued, "been using it in weapons that can de-power the Venatori without killing them or using large, messy static-field grenades. Anyhow, if set off, the microexplosive would make her useless to the Venatori, and that would probably be a death sentence unto itself. So, she agreed to return to France under the pretense of having escaped from us and feed information back to our HQ."

Bailey's eyes widened. "That's a hell of an elaborate scheme. You guys seem to get the best toys before everyone else does."

"Yeah," said the agent. "Anyway, we heard back from her right before the disaster last night. It seems that leadership of the Order is no longer in mortal hands. This ancient pagan witch-goddess, Aradia, has returned and seized control. Now she's prodding them to keep fighting and make themselves supreme among casters. It isn't just about you guys—meaning shifters—anymore. Aradia thinks that although they're extremists, the Venatori should reign as the primary power among witchkind. After what happened a couple of weeks ago, they've lost support in the larger community. This goddess feels they ought to take it back and more, through force if necessary. That includes continuing and winning the war against Weres, starting with you."

Fenris was silent throughout the man's monologue. He brooded, deep in thought.

"To achieve their aims, the Venatori, under Aradia's new war plan, are going to hit hard, hit fast, and hit first. The witch we turned wasn't high-ranking enough to sit on their top-level war councils, so we don't have the full details, but we know that something is coming and soon. Based on the last two nights, I'd say it's begun. Surgical strikes against important Weres. They seem to be targeting alphas, and acquaintances or helpers of alphas that are close to you."

Bailey clenched her hands into fists. "Shit. I don't want a full-on war either, but if they think they can pick off my friends and allies, they've got another think coming."

Velasquez stood up. "Come up with a plan on your end, and keep us informed of what you aim to do. Here's my number." He handed her a slip of paper. "I've got to get back to our side of the fight. We might be able to mitigate the worst of this, but things will escalate further. That's inescapable now. I can't promise I won't go the way of Spall or be out of the game for a while like Townsend."

Bailey frowned. She hadn't talked to Townsend recently, although she'd thanked him for his help last time she saw him.

"And to be honest," the agent admitted, "I kind of like being alive and mostly unhurt."

CHAPTER FOUR

The quartet ate the rest of their lunch without speaking after Agent Velasquez had departed. When they were done, Bailey leaned back, craving another orange soda. "They know how to make a good cheesesteak, I gotta say."

"Agreed." Roland wrapped up the third of his he'd been unable to eat and stuck it in Gunney's fridge. "Now, about this brilliant plan the Agency apparently wants us to come up with. Fenris, you got anything? It's not like you were distracted by the bodily needs of us mere mortals."

The deity was never seen eating, although Bailey somehow suspected he hunted game in the woods on his own time. He rubbed his whiskery chin and looked at the werewitch.

She cleared her throat. "If you were waiting for me to ask you the same thing, I hereby do so. What would you suggest? I have my share of ideas, but there isn't one that seems better than the others. I can't make up my mind to focus on the short term, long term, or medium term. Hell,

I'm the official shaman of the Hearth Valley, but I haven't spent a single full damn day fulfilling my duties. I was on vacation, and I've been doing other shit since then."

Part of her was embarrassed to ask. *Don't be stupid, Bailey,* she told herself. *Nobody's perfect, and you know that Fenris isn't going to give you crap for wanting advice and encouragement. He's the one who trained you.*

The tall man stood up. "You are on the right track."

"I am? Well, *that's* good, not that I was aware of it." She ran a hand through her long brown hair and tried to be optimistic that they'd figure things out.

"Yes," said Fenris. "What you said about short term versus long term, I mean. You need a plan for now, another plan for later, and a final one for the endgame. As long as you have an idea of what each one is, it's a matter of starting out with the most immediate one, leveraging your actions toward the longer-term goal, and then adapting the details as the situation changes."

She put her hands on her hips. "That makes sense, I suppose. And I'm thinking the first thing we should probably do is send word to all the pack alphas in the area to watch their backs."

"I concur." Fenris stepped closer to the girl, his somber face as unreadable as always. "Spreading word is a wise first step. The rumors are probably getting around by now, but hearing confirmation from you will put a lot of minds at ease. Even if the situation is disturbing and dangerous, it will help for them to know the facts rather than the distorted gossip."

Roland sighed. "It's too bad there isn't a 'corporate board of werewolves' so we could just send out a memo to everyone. Maybe that could be part of the longer-term plan."

"Maybe," Bailey conceded. "But I've got phone numbers for a lot of alphas, so I'll send them a group text and tell them to repeat my words *exactly* to anyone they think ought to know. That'll cut down on the urban legend bullshit."

"Or rural," Roland quipped.

Bailey punched him lightly on the arm. "Notwithstanding the smartass remarks. Next, I'd say we ought to use magic, including some from witches who are on our side to give them a horse in the race. They can track the Venatori and get an idea of their next move, something like that, so we can prepare to defend. Or go after them and drive them right the hell out of America before they can do anything else."

Fenris nodded. "Good. That might be difficult, but it is worth a try."

"And," Roland added, stretching his legs as he stood up, "I might be able to get a sampling of Seattle casters to cooperate since it seems like most of them aren't happy about the nightclub incidents. No one who frequents the party scene wants to worry about getting blown up when they're trying to get blown out or simply blown."

"Charming," snarked Bailey. "But good idea. That leaves the endgame. I'm not sure what that would entail. What's our major goal at this point? How do we win the war?"

Fenris glanced to either side as though concerned that bystanders might overhear what he was preparing to say. "I'm afraid I can answer that question."

"*Can?*" She was confused. "Are you sure you didn't mean *can't?*"

"I am sure. From what Agent Velasquez said, we might have *already* won the war if not for the Order's sudden change in leadership. They'd never admit defeat no matter what, but the Venatori might well have slunk back to their lairs and pretended that they would strike back one day to save face with their supporters while doing nothing. But with Aradia involved…"

A pit opened in Bailey's stomach and her palms sweated. She suspected the shaman's next words would not be something she would enjoy hearing.

"Our endgame plans must involve being ready to take on a goddess and ensuring that you know how to kill one."

Bailey rolled her head around her shoulders and threw up her hands. She'd never been openly sarcastic or rebellious with her teacher before, but today seemed like a good day to start.

"Kill a goddess? For fuck's sake. I'm a mortal, werewitch or no. *Can* a deity be killed?" It was crazy to think they were discussing such a thing.

Roland fidgeted. "Gods can die. Not *easily,* but it's possible."

"He's right." Fenris grunted. "We are not invulnerable. But aside from the challenge of overcoming a deity's enormous power, there is another danger."

Bailey grimaced. "Let me guess. Blowback from the divine community."

"Exactly." The tall man turned his eyes skyward, and he spoke as if from a great distance. "One cannot commit deicide without attracting a substantial amount of attention, which may come in the form of wrathful retaliation or at least heavy suspicion. It would make life more complicated, but under the circumstances, it might be necessary."

Gunney, watching and listening with mouth agape, just shook his head.

"Fine," said Bailey. "After we do the first couple of things I said, I guess it's back to training. Teach me how, and I'll kill a goddess if I have to."

Fenris gazed at her. "Good. When we have time, I will show you. One other thing first, though. We will also need to alleviate the potential hostile reaction from unaligned witches. Most of them are unaware of Aradia's return, and we cannot yet prove the link to the Venatori. So, if you were to kill a goddess of witchkind, it might appear you'd done so without provocation. That would give credence to the Venatori's slanderous insistence that you want to destroy or subjugate them all."

"Shit," Bailey mumbled, tapping her lips. "Yeah, I didn't think about that. We're gonna have to play this smart. The last thing we need is more people against us. There's got to be a way to unify some of the witch community behind us. That's our best defense, I'd think."

Roland put his hand on her shoulder. "I'm healed now, back to a hundred percent. I'll do what I can on that front."

Fenris walked away from the shop. "I will find you soon. There are things I must look into, however briefly. Warn the alphas and speak to the witches. Then we'll reconvene, and perhaps reinforce the message to the other packs with a personal visit. Or several."

Bailey and Roland made ready to fulfill their respective

obligations. Before they could leave, Gunney took the werewitch aside.

"Hey," he told her, "be careful, huh? I know I always say that, but it's worth repeating. Especially after what I heard today. Never thought I'd honestly say I was *dumbfounded* by a conversation, but there's no other word for what you guys just discussed. But even if you do end up fighting a goddess, bring your ass back in one piece."

They hugged, holding each other tight for nearly half a minute.

"That's the plan, old man. I haven't come back in multiple pieces yet."

"Good." He released her, then fished in his pocket for a set of keys, the ones to the hot rod they'd been restoring. "Being alive has its perks. I ain't gonna *give* it to you since I already gave you the damn Camaro, but I figure you can borrow it at least. Deal?"

She laughed. "Deal."

<hr>

The alpha of the Hemlock Valley pack and his two main lieutenants stood with arms folded in a posture of vague standoffishness, their jaws gradually falling open as they listened to the tall tale being related by the girl who'd stepped out of a glowing portal.

"So," Bailey concluded, "make no mistake, they're coming. What happened in Seattle wasn't a fluke. I haven't met you guys in person before, but I do recall you sent me an email saying you'd help me out if I ever made it up to Canada. Well, I have, and now I'm gonna help *you* out."

Fenris and Roland, standing at her elbows, nodded solemnly in agreement. Her mind took a short detour to wonder if Roland had ever been into British Columbia before. She didn't think he had, despite living only a short distance from the border.

"So," Bailey went on, "keep your people in tight and stay wary. Everybody needs to keep an eye on everyone else. Don't go out alone, whether in the wilderness or the city, anywhere you're vulnerable or cut off from help. Travel in large groups and check in regularly. Stuff like that. It's not much, but it'll go a long way toward stopping the Venatori from picking off all our alphas and warriors. They'll have to concentrate on one target at a time, bringing all their witches to bear at once instead of making a bunch of simultaneous strikes against multiple people."

"Okay." The alpha frowned, his eyebrows twitching along his brow. He wasn't hostile toward her unexpected visit, exactly, just flummoxed by the situation. "What's this stuff about a goddess? Sorry, but I have to ask."

Roland whispered, "Why did he say 'sorry?' It must be true what they say about Canadians."

Bailey elbowed him in the ribs and replied, "We've got credible information that says the Venatori are now being led by an ancient goddess of witchcraft who wants them to keep trying to wipe us out, and me in particular. That's serious business, but we're working on a way to counter it. It helps that we have a god of our own, of course, even if he can't intervene directly on our behalf."

The Hemlock Valley Weres conferred among themselves for a minute. It sounded like they were debating whether they believed the stuff about Aradia, although

Bailey was fairly sure they'd gotten the point about the rest.

The werewitch added, "I know it sounds crazy, but we've all seen things lately that we would never have expected to see in ten lifetimes, haven't we? If we're not careful, we could end up in a full-on war. A proxy struggle between gods."

Stating it that way, she wondered if Fenris would disapprove. He hadn't indicated, as far as she could recall, that he harbored any bitterness toward the other deities. He'd even sort of patched things up with Freya.

The huddle ended, and the alpha faced her again. "All right, we'll take your advice and be damn careful for a while. Most everything we've heard about you has been good, Bailey. We've got no reason to distrust you, but it's hard to believe some of this stuff."

Admitting they had a point, Bailey bade them farewell. Then she, the wizard, and the god-shaman stepped back through the purple gateway and vanished.

They emerged in the Other, the parallel dimension formed of the mortal world's magical runoff, which functioned as a hub from which they could open multiple portals and skip from place to place.

So far, they'd been to nine different packs throughout the Pacific Northwest—Oregon, Washington, and southwestern Canada. They had determined that the packs who were closest to Bailey—the South Cliffs, the Silver Stars, and the Junipers, among others—would heed her text warning without extra encouragement, but it seemed wise to visit the others in person. The Hemlocks had been last on the list.

After the portal's cold, dizzying sensation faded, they stepped out into the dim, boggy swamps and woods and misty heaths of the Other.

Roland let out a dramatic exhalation. "I'm glad that's over. I swear, I get, like, jet lag or something from portal-hopping. Even when it's across lines of longitude rather than latitude, for whatever reason."

"You're weird," Bailey teased. "Anyway, yeah, I think the wolves of the Northwest are about as prepared as they're gonna get. What now, Fenris? Do we start my training on how to kill a goddess?"

She had to admit she was curious to the point of excitement. The sheer audacity and insanity of the prospect had piqued her curiosity.

Having fought mortal mages who were terrifyingly powerful enough, she knew that what they were considering was nothing to fuck around with.

Fenris considered his words before he spoke. "We mentioned to the various pack alphas that the Other could, if necessary, act as a safe haven and an emergency refuge site. Now that I think about it, it could be far more than that."

Roland winced. "Uh-oh. Any time he has an 'idea' involving the Other, it usually involves us having to hang out for three days in here fighting consecutive armies of ghosts, demons, angels, will o' the wisps, shoggoths, and gods know what else. Am I right?"

"No," Fenris stated. "Only an army of witches."

The wizard pursed his lips. "Well, *that* comes as a relief. Witches we can handle, mostly."

The deity elaborated. "The Venatori view you, Bailey, as

the single greatest threat to their supremacy. You are an extremely powerful caster, and one who, not being a member of the witch species, falls outside their control. I suspect that their attacks on alphas are designed to cripple your support structure and deprive you of powerful allies. It's a temporary digression. Their priority is your destruction, and that means wherever you go, they will follow."

The proverbial light bulb went off in her head. "Use the Other as a giant trap for them, you mean. I like it. They sure as hell have it coming."

"That," Fenris agreed, "but it also moves the fighting away from civilian populations. The witch cult's methods are growing even more ruthless and erratic. The more we have to confront them on Earth, the more chance there is for casualties among innocent witches or normal humans."

Bailey gave a sharp nod. "Yeah, definitely. More of them are filtering into the country, though, and plotting their next strike. If we're going to lure them in here for an ambush, we need to set it up and then spring it as soon as we can. Think we should involve the pack alphas?"

Roland pointed out, "If we don't, the Venatori might focus on wiping them out while we're 'hiding' in the Other. Of course, if we bring a small army in here, they might suspect an ambush. So, I dunno."

Silence settled over the bog as Fenris mulled it over. "Involve the alphas. I'll open a portal to Greenhearth so you can send them another group text to inform them of the plan all at once, not to mention check on the town. Then we'll start gathering them, leaving breadcrumbs to bait the witches into the trap."

"Good deal." Bailey frowned. "I forgot to call my

brothers before we went portal-hopping anyway. They're gonna be pissed."

They'd spent only an hour back home before warping back into the Other. Bailey had made sure everyone was all right and things were still quiet. Her brothers forgave her, under the circumstances.

Then they'd contacted all the alphas throughout the region. Most of them were keeping their phones close, and it didn't take long to receive replies. All agreed to the plan, but only four could come right away. The rest asked if they could meet up tomorrow and have today to get things in order with their homes.

"Consider," Roland suggested as they languished near the pole barn behind the Nordin house, "that we did tell them to make changes with how their whole packs behave. And the Venatori usually pause before their next strike after they hit a snag like they did in Tacoma. I'd say our friends ought to be okay overnight. We can collect them in the morning."

The werewitch agreed. "So be it. And if the Venatori *do* strike, they've been warned." Specifically, the packs were to text Bailey right away, so that she and Fenris could open a portal to evacuate them.

Fenris looked around as if feeling the air. "We have the evening to make preparations of our own, then. I suggest we return to the Other for a short time. Remember that time passes more slowly there, so we will not be gone long enough to miss any emergency messages should they come in."

"Okay." Bailey shrugged. "It would help if we at least could decide where to set the ambush and roughly how to go about it."

"We will," the shaman assured her. "And we should also begin your training for the endgame."

He turned, raised his hands, spoke a brief incantation, and opened a shimmering doorway in the air before him. Bailey and Roland stepped through, with the god following them.

They emerged in a different part of the Other than the nondescript swamp area they'd used as their teleportation hub. It was, however, familiar.

The ground was higher and somewhat rocky, and the trees were tall and lush. Silver moonlight so bright it was like noon shone on them. At the top of the gradual ridge, the temple of her people's shamans awaited. They'd come to the holy ground of the lycanthropic people.

"Here?" Bailey asked. "It's probably a good idea. They'll think we're like mice fleeing to someplace we feel safe, when in fact, we're cats getting ready to pounce."

Fenris grunted. "This is where we'll set the trap. We have a natural advantage here. But before we delve into the specifics of that, I feel you must have a basic understanding of how a deity can be destroyed. You won't be called upon to fight Aradia yet, but the sooner you grasp the fundamentals of it, the better."

Roland gave a low whistle. "This ought to be good. There are old myths and legends of mighty heroes who struck down gods with enchanted weapons and stuff like that, but I assumed they were metaphorical. Though we *do* have records of divine beings ceasing to exist."

The tall shaman's face seemed darker and more brooding than usual beneath his hood, and he waved a hand sharply.

"It can only be done with magic," he began. "No mortal weapon can accomplish the deed."

Bailey leaned forward. Her skin prickled as she listened.

"Only powerful witches or wizards, or werewitches, possess the requisite power. Most were-shamans lack the arcane capacity for deicide. Other supernatural creatures who possess a handful of magical tricks or humans who've managed to unlock a small portion of the occult have never demonstrated the necessary strength. A god such as I has the power, but for me to kill Aradia would start a war of the divine, which could unmake the world. In other words, Bailey, you are one of the few people who has a chance."

She swallowed a mouthful of spit.

"It's extremely dangerous," Fenris continued. "Even if you're successful, the process involves levels of power few beings are equipped to handle."

Roland leaned in next to her and held her hand. She knew for all that he was worried about her, his bump of intellectual curiosity had to be practically drooling right now about hearing the highest secrets of magic.

"What you must do," the tall man said and spread his hands, each forming a sort of claw, "is to perform a ritual that will create a conduit between you and the witch-goddess. Then you must *ground* it the way you would a lightning rod and open up a transference of power, much like using jumper cables on a car battery. From there, you have two options."

He makes it sound so simple, Bailey mused. *I kinda suspect, though, that the reality isn't going to be that straightforward.*

"First, you can bleed her dry. Allow her magic to dissipate into the surrounding universe so that she weakens to the point of ceasing to exist. That, however, carries the danger of doing damage to the rest of the world. Not to mention, she can retaliate as she's dying."

Bailey squinted. "Sounds like that'd be Plan B, then."

"Perhaps," Fenris acceded. "But the other method has its risks as well. That one involves using yourself as a vessel for the drained power. You would essentially vampirize her, stealing her strength and directing it back against her while she is weakened. It would allow you to eliminate her more quickly. But..."

Roland sighed. "Here we go with the proviso."

"There are many ways it could go wrong on your end, all of which would kill you."

She looked at the ground and prodded a rock with the tip of her boot. "Well, that sucks, too."

Fenris shook his head. "There is no easy way. If you adopt the second method, you might absorb too much of the goddess' magic at once, which would be like setting off a nuclear bomb within yourself. Or you might fail to absorb enough, which would neither weaken Aradia sufficiently nor give you enough power to kill her. The task will balance on the edge of a knife, no matter how you approach it. But I can help prepare you."

Having concluded his spiel, he motioned for her to sit cross-legged against a tree, and meditate on all he'd said.

"Soon," he added, "we will return to Greenhearth to ensure nothing's happened while we've been gone. But for now, relax your mind and open it as wide as you can. You're going to need to broaden your horizons beyond anything you've done before if you intend to act as a receptacle for the ultimate power of the universe."

CHAPTER FIVE

Most of the alphas and lieutenants had never been into the Other in any capacity, let alone the part of it that was the sacred territory of their race.

"Wow," one of them breathed, his eyes as big as golf balls.

Bailey and Fenris had brought them right to the edge of the enchanted forest. They were still a fair distance from the temple, but here was where the holy ground began. It was more rugged than the rest of the Other, but also far more beautiful—a wolves' paradise of lush wilderness beneath a perpetually full moon.

Their god stepped forth and raised his arms to summon their attention. "My children," he proclaimed, "this place has long stood as our one unassailable sanctuary. And yet, only two weeks ago, it *was* assailed by our deadly enemies, the Venatori. It is fitting that our plan is to lure them here again. It shall become their graveyard. We will fertilize our hallowed soil with their corpses."

Bailey tried not to frown. *That's a damn harsh way of*

putting it. It's true, but still. We're not the bloodthirsty ones here. We're just defending ourselves from their crazy-ass schemes. But leave it to Fenris to get a reaction out of the boys.

Hearing their deity speak, the warriors instantly got over their slack-jawed wonder and took to pumping fists in the air and cheering. There was a vicious edge to it that Bailey didn't much like, but it meant they were ready to fight.

As they needed to be.

Bailey took a step forward. "Okay, we're going to go over the basics of the plan, and then we'll move on to the details of what each of you will be doing. Understood?"

They all nodded or grunted.

"Good. Simply put, the gist is that we make it too hard for them to attack our people back on Earth by making sure they're always in large groups or someplace in public where the police would get involved right away, stuff like that. Not to mention, all the high-value targets—meaning you guys and me—will conveniently be glimpsed 'fleeing' into the Other. So, they take account of their choices and decide the best thing to do is chase us in here—where we'll have pockets of Weres set up waiting for them, and a few other tricks up our sleeves. Then we kick their asses so hard, they have no choice but to abandon their crusade against us once and for all."

She left out the part about drawing Aradia into the battle and destroying her. The Weres knew the goddess was involved in the current shenanigans. For all their courage, they didn't need to test it by ruminating on a battle in which a deity might personally participate.

Fenris took over the next stage of the briefing. "This

spot will be the staging point. When you pretend to take cover, you will arrive right here. Then you'll move up the slope into these woods. We will have the advantage here. It won't take long to put them on the defensive."

The Hemlocks' alpha raised a beefy hand. "Sorry, but how is this place better than our own home forests? Do we get, say, a magical bonus here?"

The tall shaman's mouth twisted into the faint shadow of a smile. "Not exactly. Rather, the opposite. The Other naturally imposes limits on casters' channeling of arcane power. Granted, the Venatori are skilled enough that most of them can operate at nearly full potential, but even a slight dampening of their magic's potency will work to our benefit. Furthermore, destructive spells are easier to cast in open terrain. In the woods, we, when shifted, will be more maneuverable since this is our element. We also possess senses sharper than those of any witch. We'll use guerilla tactics, hit-and-run, to wear them down and finally crush them."

Fenris led the whole group up the forested slope as he and Bailey went into more detail about the roles each Were would play. They familiarized themselves with the terrain as they walked, and most of them shifted into wolf form to get a feel for the ground, the trees, and the air.

The two leaders took a short break while the wolves explored. Fenris looked at Bailey. "You seem distracted. Is something wrong?"

There was no point in lying. "I'm worried about Roland, mainly. He's walking alone into the lion's den. Everyone's going to be on edge after what went down two nights back. But then again," she acknowledged, rubbing her nose, "it's his goddamn hometown."

———

"Listen," Roland urged, holding his hands out in front of him in a gesture meant to emphasize how exasperated he was getting, "I'm from here, okay? My family is the living equivalent of a Seattle Historic Landmark. And I've been to this club, like, four or five times before. Mostly when I was younger, but still. I just want to know if everyone is okay and ask them what the hell happened."

The proprietor was a vampire named DeMornay who, having chosen a building in which to house his establishment that was easy to sun-proof, kept unusual hours for his kind. Apparently he often awoke at three or four in the afternoon, and then did not go to sleep until a couple hours *past* dawn.

Such were the ways in which ancient creatures had adapted to the modern world.

"I understand," DeMornay drawled, his basso profundo voice clashing with his thin, effete appearance, "and I do remember you. Somewhat. But for safety reasons, I can't divulge much of my clients' personal information right now. The mass murder has left people rather jumpy. It's been bad enough for business as it is. Violating the well-established protocols of confidentiality would drive customers away when I can't afford to lose them."

Sighing, Roland admitted defeat. "Fine. May I at least see the place? For old time's sake, I guess. I could use a drink, anyway."

The vampire gave a dry chuckle. "Of course. I never said you couldn't *attend* the club. Granted, we technically do not open until nightfall, but I've been known to make exceptions. Welcome back."

He admitted the wizard and served him a basic but refreshing Screwdriver, then returned to readying himself for the night.

Roland looked around as he sipped his drink. Besides him, the only other "exceptions" were a young couple, probably witches, who paid him no attention while they swigged from bottles of hard lemonade and chatted in low voices.

A couple of the rails, he saw, were still broken. And they hadn't yet fully removed the bloodstains from the floor.

Roland wandered over to the couple. "Hi," he opened. "Pardon the interruption, but I used to come here all the time, and I've been trying to figure out what happened. The reports have all contradicted each other."

They looked up at him with annoyance through half-lidded eyes. The girl was definitely a witch. Her dress was old-fashioned and semi-formal, not quite a RomantiGoth style, but close. The guy was more the type who did not wear cloth sleeves, the better to show off his sleeves of ink. Roland was pretty sure he was a mundane human, albeit one who was "in the know" about the supernatural. DeMornay would never have admitted a Muggle.

"Umm," the girl said, "my friend Sheila posted the video, like, everywhere. Look it up." She turned back to her date, and both ignored him.

Nodding, Roland took a quick tour of the bloodstains,

finished his beverage, and showed himself to the door. Once he was outside, he turned his face to the heavens.

"This," he murmured, "is why I left Seattle."

He checked his phone and looked up the names of the Weres who'd been killed. He could find out more from the witch community by hitting up some of his old friends, but right now, it seemed more important to reach out to the local shifters. Chances were, tensions were already near the boiling point.

Among the victims was a local werewolf named Greg Holmquist who'd been well-liked. If Roland were to speak to his family, word would get around.

The wizard used a combination of inside sources, obscure Internet forums, magic, and the slight hacking skills he'd developed over the years to procure an address. The Holmquists lived in Fremont—not far, in fact, from the Troll, or from the library where he and Bailey had spent an afternoon perusing the "special" collection.

"Off we go," he remarked and caught the first bus.

Twenty-five minutes later, he stood before the small blue bungalow with the correct number out front, knocked on the door, and waited. A minute passed, then footsteps approached, and a short, tired-looking woman with red-rimmed eyes opened the main door a crack, leaving the screen door shut.

"Hello?" she asked.

"Hi. I've come to apologize for what happened, on behalf of myself, the rest of my kind, and Bailey Nordin, if you've heard of her. My name is Roland. I'm a Seattle native, although I've been away from home."

The woman, probably Greg's mother, at first stared at

him open-mouthed in a kind of dull shock, as though multiple emotions were fighting for control of her reaction and she could not choose between them.

"You're a wizard," she declared.

"Yes. I came back after I heard about the recent tragedy. It...depressed me greatly, especially since the Venatori do *not* speak for all of us. Hell, I'm *dating* a Were. I just wanted to offer my condolences and my support, if you're willing to have it."

Again the woman seemed unable to know how to react. She looked aside for a moment, swallowed a lump in her throat, and then fixed him with a keen stare. "How do you know Bailey?"

"She's the one I'm dating," he replied. "Here's a picture of us." He showed her a photo on his phone of the two of them biting into an extra-long steak sandwich at a restaurant in Boise.

The woman stared at it for a full minute. "Okay. You can come inside if you want. Coffee?"

"Yes, please." He followed her in.

The house was dim and basic but cozy. Roland was surprised to discover five more people within, all Weres, sitting in a circle in the living room. Mrs. Holmquist introduced them: her husband, sister, and two other children, as well as a neighbor who'd stopped over to talk. They all looked at him with frosty uncertainty.

He repeated what he'd said to the woman, elaborating upon the basic theme of how the Venatori's atrocities did not represent all of witchkind, and how he and Bailey were on their side. Once they started to warm up to him, he also repeated Bailey's warning that the Venatori would soon return, and the importance of being prepared.

"She's working with Fenris right now," he explained, "on a plan to lure them into a trap and put an end to their little campaign once and for all. And if you or any other Weres throughout the Pacific Northwest need help, call out to Fenris. He'll open a portal and ferry you into the Other —the parallel dimension we use to travel from place to place—where we'll have a bunch of fighters waiting. They won't catch us unaware again."

The group digested his spiel. After a moment, Mr. Holmquist looked the wizard in the eye.

"You," he began in a gravelly voice, "are the first caster to have reached out to us. We expect nothing from witches, Venatori or no. If you and Bailey are together, perhaps that explains it, but...thank you. We'll do as she recommends."

Roland smiled. "No, thank *you*."

He took his leave, confident that things had gone well, and that the Holmquists would disperse the message throughout Seattle. Urban lycanthropes tended to be more assimilated into society than rural ones, which made them harder to pinpoint even for Fenris.

"Now," the wizard groaned, "on to building the other half of the bridge."

Which meant talking to his own kind. He didn't relish the prospect.

Witches his age or younger tended to be sarcastic, elitist, shallow, and totally devoid of wisdom regardless of their intelligence or magical ability. He decided, therefore, that it would be better to aim his diplomatic efforts at the community's elders. Some of them would remember him since he'd been popular as a kid.

"Oh, God," he gasped, a cold wave of nausea striking him as an especially unpleasant thought intruded upon his brain. "What if I run into *Shannon?*"

He wracked his brain for recent information on the subject of his longtime stalker.

When he'd called or texted his family and old friends, they hadn't mentioned her, so that was encouraging. Perhaps with her friends Aida and Callie dead and herself beaten and humiliated, Shannon had given up and left Seattle, moving on to greener pastures where she'd find a nice man to marry. One who had a thing for batshit-crazy women.

He strolled toward the nearest bus stop. "But when have things ever been that easy?"

Thus far, things *had* been easy, in that the dreaded Ms. DiGrezza hadn't shown up. But in all other respects, they'd been pretty fucking difficult.

"So, by all means," Roland concluded, with a dramatic flourish of his hand, "if you want to wreck your city and country, lose the respect of your neighbors, and quite possibly get yourselves killed while you're at it, help the Venatori next time they show up. But if any of those things sound like they might be bad ideas, bar your doors and put some headphones on when they knock on your door. If you can't or won't join us, at least *don't* join *them.*"

The dozen witches sitting around the table stared at

him with eyes like polished stones. It wasn't that they disagreed, or that they were likely to jump in on the attempted were-genocide or anything of the sort. Or so it seemed to him.

No, the reason for their chilly reception was far more infuriating in Roland's mind.

They thought he was being rude by bringing it up.

He'd managed to convene the twelve of them in a private dining room at a hotel his family occasionally patronized. Sitting before him at the moment were some of the leading lights of Seattle's sorcerous community, all older folks, nine females and three males. He knew eight of the women and two of the men.

Their leader was Mrs. Noreen Ashbury, who'd always sort of reminded Roland of the evil stepmother from the Disney animated *Cinderella*. She wasn't evil, and her wardrobe was a bit more up to date, but those were the only minor differences.

"Roland," she said, as though addressing a child, "we appreciate your passion and enthusiasm. However, the matters of which you speak are ultimately of minimal concern to us. The Venatori are distasteful people, but if there were a legitimate threat against us from the lycanthropes, we might conceivably agree to a marriage of convenience with them."

His stomach roiled at that.

"But," Ashbury went on, "your recent scry-broadcast made clear what we'd suspected, namely that the Order is once again attempting to drum up public support for one of their crazed endeavors. They tried something similar years before you were born on a smaller scale."

The wizard blinked. "I did not know that."

"You're young," she stated as though that explained everything, and took a sip of tea. "It's true that there's been a distressing flare-up of violence lately. Yet in many ways, this seems like business as usual. The affairs of werewolves, meanwhile, are not a primary concern of ours. Yes, we'd prefer they not be exterminated, but if this is just a feud, then it's up to them to fight."

Roland felt his face taking on a curdled expression of resignation. The meeting was shaping up to be a Pyrrhic victory. Seattle's elder witches were evincing no interest in joining the enemy, but equally little concern for helping Bailey.

Then Mrs. Ashbury raised a finger in an imperious gesture that drew his attention. "There is one other thing, though," she added.

"Oh?" He had a bad feeling about this.

"Tell us," the older woman insisted, "what you've heard about the goddess Aradia supposedly manifesting to sponsor the Venatori's efforts."

Shit, Roland thought.

"Uh," he responded, "based on everything I've seen and heard, it's possible. I haven't seen Aradia, but I *did* see Freya. Twice. The first time was a couple of months back, and you all presumably saw her yourselves during the broadcast. That was the second time. So if nothing else, I'll be the first to admit that yes, the gods are real. But we all know how trustworthy the Venatori are. They might be claiming to have a deity on their side as yet another propaganda venture."

Mrs. Ashbury frowned, and the other elders mimicked the expression.

"I see," she said, her tone neutral. "Young though you are, you've always shown signs of intelligence. What is your opinion of Freya's role in this? And, if she exists, Aradia's?"

He'd have to speak carefully. He cleared his throat and rustled his hair to stall for time.

"Freya," he opined, "is a stern goddess, but she probably has our best interests at heart. I can't speak for other deities, though. The old legends about them having much the same personality quirks and selfish traits as humans seem to be true. On some level, the divine hosts have their own motives. They care more about our veneration and our obedience to their goals than they do about *us* for our own sake. With Aradia, who can say?"

One of the older wizards scowled at his borderline blasphemy, and the women didn't look comfortable, either.

Ashbury finished her tea and set down the saucer. "Very well, then. I'd say this meeting is adjourned. Thank you, Roland, for making us aware of what is going on. We cannot pledge any support toward your new friends, but we can, if nothing else, help you by staying out of the way."

"I'll take what I can get." He shrugged.

Being younger and faster, he was out the hotel's front door before the rest of them had departed the dining room. As he paused for a breath of fresh air on the sidewalk, he realized that a young man was looking at him.

"Hi," Roland said. "Do I know you? You seem vaguely familiar."

The guy stepped closer. "I think we've met once or

twice. You're Roland, right? I'm Dante Viari. I, ah, I was at the club."

Roland examined the young wizard. The two of them weren't dissimilar. Dante, like himself, was thin and blond, with a shock of pale hair that hung down over his face. He was pale and green-eyed, an inch or two shorter than Roland, and perhaps three or four years younger, which would make him approximately twenty-five. He wore a tight black turtleneck and equally tight jeans.

The wizards shook hands.

"At the club, you say?" Roland quipped. "Well, then unless you're a psychopath who's preparing to knife me in the back, I probably don't need to convince you that the Venatori suck."

"No," Dante muttered, "you don't. My friend Liam was one of the guys they murdered. I, uh, I've heard of you and Bailey. Things are so tense and crazy right now that I've been keeping things on the down-low, but..."

The young man, who seemed on the shy and awkward side, steeled himself. "I want to join up. They have to pay for that shit. I don't care what any of those people said." He waved a hand toward the hotel.

The other wizard nodded, impressed. "And here was me, thinking I'd have better luck recruiting from among the old farts. They don't want to be involved in the situation at all. The whole thing isn't *respectable*." He sneered the word. "Anyway, I'm sorry about your friend, but I'm glad you're on board."

"Yeah." Dante looked around. "I have an idea for how we might be able to rally more witches to our side. Want to get a drink?"

"Sure, as long as it's alcoholic."

Agent Velasquez checked the time and waited for his man to report back. If he didn't hear back from him within one minute, they'd have to move in, despite the risks.

The condominium building rose unobtrusively from a cluster of palms in Northeast Los Angeles, and little about it was different from the other residential properties in the neighborhood. Pedestrians strolled by now and again, and cars zipped along and honked on the nearby major street, but the agents were well-hidden from view.

He took a deep breath. This was his first time commanding a squad. Though still only a Junior Agent, manpower shortages combined with his good track record under Townsend had propelled him into a leadership role in the man's absence. Townsend's recommendation that he take over hadn't hurt either.

"All right," he began, "we–"

"*Sir.*" The voice had come through their headsets. It was Agent Glover.

Velasquez motioned for everyone to keep silent. "We were two seconds away from continuing without you. What's the report?"

"About what we expected, sir," the voice replied. "Seven of them in the penthouse on top. Otherwise, the building is damn near empty. Basic support staff and that's about it. Currently, there's only the maintenance guy in the northeast corner of the first floor."

Velasquez exhaled through his nose, relieved that the

force was no larger than they'd anticipated. "Roger. We'll meet you on the way in. Over and out."

The squad fired up their noise inhibitors, cocooning themselves in a transparent shell of sound-proof arcane energy, and entered the condo through its rear entrance. Glover had disabled both the building's regular alarms and the warning glyphs the witches had planted. Velasquez suspected that the Venatori would grow more clever in how they protected themselves soon since the Agency had thus far managed to break through most of the tricks they used.

Once inside, Agent Glover rejoined them from under the stairwell. They tramped upward, moving fast and only hesitating long enough to check above them with mirrors and portable sonar devices. The noise inhibitors masked the racket of their boots on the steps, so that was one thing they needn't worry about.

They double-checked the exact positions of the sorceresses before they burst through the door, arcanoplasm rifles held ready to kill.

Glowing magenta-white beams streaked across the penthouse as agents dashed in, their movements disciplined and merciless. Two of the three witches in the main living area screamed as the blazing projectiles vaporized them. The third they left alone.

Then they moved on to the rest. Since the other three had had a second or two's notice, they were able to counterattack, and two men took light to moderate wounds from elemental spells. But their shields and knives neutralized most of the magic, and in seconds, the remaining Venatori joined their comrades in hell.

The last of the ashes settled as half of the agents fanned out through the penthouse to check for any stragglers. Velasquez was among those who remained in the main room.

Along with the one survivor.

She was a fortyish woman, attractive but for her sullen face, and she stood among the remains of her fellows with a tightly-wound, nervous placidity.

Velasquez caught her eyes. "Madame Dormois. You're not hurt, are you? Thanks again for all your help."

"No," she said, "I am fine. And you are welcome." Her tone was too monotone to be sincere, but thus far, she'd given them no reason to suspect insubordination. It would have been extremely unwise for her to turn triple-agent.

"Good." Velasquez took her to the far corner, away from the other men as well as the windows. "Tell me every- thing I need to know about what your Order has been up to since you went back to France. We received your message about Aradia and have been preparing accord- ingly. Now, we want to know about troop movements, step-by-step plans, and all that juicy stuff."

The woman inhaled and moved her shoulders to gather her thoughts and prepare to translate them into English.

Before she could speak, Velasquez added, "And remem- ber, if anything you say turns out to be a lie..." He raised a hand and flicked his fingers outwards in all directions while mouthing the word *Boom.*

The witch narrowed her eyes. "I know that!" she snapped.

Then, forcing herself to calm down, she delivered her report. "War-witches of the Venatori have infiltrated every major American city, along with some of the smaller ones in strategic locations. Most of the groups are small, ten or fewer, the better for them to blend in and flee to disappear if they are discovered. But others are larger if there are more wolves in an area. Groups of up to three dozen. They are making very precise strikes against lycanthropes, especially those who have pledged loyalty to Bailey Nordin."

Velasquez nodded. Most of what she'd said was redundant, but the Agency was uncertain of how widespread the Order's presence was. If indeed there were that many of them spread throughout all the big cities...

Dormois went on, "The largest concentrations, as well as the ancillary troops, are located in the Northwest. This is due to the presence of Nordin and her forces. The strategy is to eliminate her allies all over the continent while keeping her pinned down in Oregon and Washington. Soon there will be enough witches in that region to overpower any uprising or counterattack by the lycanthropes. Or so my superiors believe. They seemed very confident that we cannot be overcome this time. They have drawn upon almost all available personnel to destroy the shifters."

The agent felt his eyes going out of focus as his attention momentarily drifted to the magnitude of what their spy had said. His bosses had believed that the Venatori were on the verge of exhaustion after the last battle. In fact, they'd only begun.

And the Agency wasn't prepared to resist an invasion of that magnitude. They needed to do more ASAP.

One of Velasquez' men appeared beside him. "The

penthouse is clear. Rest of the building's secure, too. Awaiting further instructions."

He glanced over his shoulder at the man. "Make ready to leave. We'll be taking Madame Dormois with us. Ensure that no one is watching or waiting for us outside."

"Yes, sir." The team set to bustling.

Velasquez lingered. He took out his cell phone and called Bailey. No signal. He walked a few yards away, tried again, and got the same result.

"Dammit," he muttered. "She *has* to know about this. By now, we might be screwed without the Weres bolstering our numbers. Shit, we might even have to bring regular law enforcement or the goddamn National Guard into the situation."

They were having trouble keeping things quiet as it was. The Internet was abuzz with rumors being spread by the more paranoid—or observant—of the normies.

Velasquez called the agent in charge of the four-man team that was keeping an eye on Greenhearth. If necessary, they could dispatch all their operatives in Portland, although it would take about an hour to get them all to the Hearth Valley.

The call went through. "Friedman."

Velasquez stated his name, then asked, "What's the word on Bailey? Where is she?"

Friedman cleared his throat. "She's not here. We don't know where she is, but definitely not in any of her usual places around town. I already ordered an information sweep and will send you the results as soon as I get them."

"Good," responded the other agent. "Thanks. Over and out."

He turned and saw one of his men on the verge of asking if he was coming. Waving a hand, Velasquez trailed the man down to the street and climbed into one of their cars.

"Airport," he said to the driver. "Not sure where we're going yet, but we'll find out soon."

They'd commandeered a small private airfield in the lower San Gabriel Mountains. Minutes before they arrived, Friedman's message came in.

Velasquez checked his device. It seemed that a quick analysis of Internet chatter among Were-friendly sites and forums had turned up some promising info. There was mention of the Other, and a reference to keeping all shifters together in large groups for safety.

"Well, that's good," he nodded, realizing at once that the Were community was doing part of his job for him by getting ready to defend against further witch attacks. But still… His brow furrowed.

He'd heard of the Other, and the Agency had unofficially confirmed that it existed, but it was poorly understood. All they knew so far was that it was a kind of parallel universe accessible to supernatural types. If Bailey had gone there, he had no way of getting in touch with her.

The report also mentioned that Roland had been sighted in Seattle.

As the agents stepped onto the airfield, Velasquez wasted no time in preparing a flight plan to Washington State, complete with a private chopper waiting for him once he got there. No point in fighting traffic.

Bailey looked at Fenris. "Is this going to work? I mean, I'm sure it's worth a try."

"It should," the shaman stated. "You're more than talented enough to manage it."

In a circle, spread out at a safe distance, her various alphas and their lieutenants stood and watched. There were more than had been with her when they'd first come into the Other, for some had trickled in. She insisted on keeping many of them with their packs back on Earth for safety, but there were enough here to make a formidable force.

Bailey raised her hands, closed her eyes, and channeled power from the universe through her own mind.

Fenris had come up with the idea for the spell, helped somewhat by the werewitch's input, and after a period of minor testing and theorizing, they'd decided to give it a try. If it worked, they'd have a significant edge and be able to fast-track their plans, forcing the Venatori's collective hand.

She located her aura, her signature within the world of magic, and drew free-floating sources of power to it. Then she magnified it, swelling it as if adding fuel and heat to a fire.

Fenris stood by her side. "Now, concentrate," he urged. "Imagine it flowing outward from you, breaking off into separate pieces, as many as possible. And keep channeling more magic into it as it diminishes, the better to make even more copies of your astral signature."

His voice, soothing and authoritative, helped rather than distracted her. She could feel her essence expanding, and the "flares" it sent out becoming fireballs unto themselves.

"Good," Fenris complimented her. "Concentrate. Make as many as you can. And then for your alphas, too."

More magical flares erupted from her, coalescing into what her mind's eye saw as human figures of pure light and sorcery. Then she sent the arcane force out, linked it with the smaller auras of the wolves encircling her, and created similar pseudo-clones of them, as well.

Their deity did his part by opening multiple portals in sequence to allow the astral projections to step out of the Other and drift back into the mortal world.

Anyone scrying them or trying to track their magical activity would see or sense just enough to be baited by the ruse. To the witches, it would appear—if all went according to plan—that magically-empowered alphas were reinforcing their local pack communities.

And more importantly, as Bailey drew her astral clones back through the same portals to her, it would look as though she were teleporting around before fleeing back into the Other. Alone.

The tall shaman put a hand to his temple. "It's working. Yes, I can tell. I can feel their attention, their malevolent will. They are reconsidering their strikes against the packs, thinking them too large and heavily guarded. And at the same time, they've noticed you running away into this realm. The opportunity is too much to resist. They all know they would be richly rewarded for destroying the werewitch."

Bailey drew the astral doubles back toward herself,

holding them near her original aura at her current physical location.

"And," Fenris added, "they're here. About two dozen of them have filtered into the forest not far from us. Perhaps two miles on Earth."

The girl ended the spell, but when she opened her eyes and stood normally, she felt energized, as though manipulating that much power had increased her abilities and her readiness. Her alphas looked at her with eyes blazing with anticipation.

She turned to them with a bestial grin. "All right, guys," she said, "it's time to go on the hunt."

CHAPTER SIX

Dante had led Roland to a bar he'd never drunk in before. It was a newer place, and he'd been away from home for months now. Not to mention, he'd mostly stopped paying attention to the local scene even before he'd wandered off to Greenhearth.

It was furnished in a dark, swanky, garish, faintly "hip" fashion, somewhat crass and pretentious by Roland's tastes, but nice enough. The style was popular with the younger witches, and it seemed most of the clientele were part of the caster community.

Roland raised his glass. "I must say," he began, "they make a damn good mimosa. I haven't drunk many fruity mixed drinks recently, mostly beer and the occasional whiskey and Coke. Similarly," he cast his eyes down at the plate before him, "my lady friend is an enthusiast of steak sandwiches, so having a *club* sandwich with a nice sprig of parsley and all is a treat. Thanks again."

He bit into his food, relishing the taste. Since club sandwiches weren't rare or fancy, he saw no reason why the

Bristling Elk couldn't introduce them to its menu. He'd suggest it once he was back in Oregon.

Dante sipped his martini. "You're welcome. So, yeah, I know who you are and what you've been up to, and you've more than earned the cost of a decent lunch. If you're serious about rallying witches, I think we need to hit up the club scene. You'd be amazed by how many people will listen to someone who can back up his claims."

The younger wizard shrugged, then added, "By myself, no one would believe me or follow me. It's not like I'm unpopular exactly, but you have real clout."

"I do?" Roland marveled. "Earlier I was at DeMornay's place, and the couple hanging out there acted like I had crawled out of a tipped-over garbage can."

"Well, in certain circles," Dante clarified. "Like, among those who are paying attention to what's going on. There's a lot of suppressed anger against the Venatori. They're riling things up in a bad way and crashing everyone's party. Most people are too scared to do anything about it, though, what with their reputation."

The Order was a persistent source of boogeyman stories to American witches, as Roland well knew. *Don't draw too much negative attention to yourself*, their elders had implied, *or the Venatori will crawl out from under your bed and eat you.*

"But," Dante continued, "knowing that the whole were-wolf population is rallying to fight them and having confirmation that the rumors are true might be enough to tip the scales. I think a lot of us would join up if we knew we wouldn't have to do it alone and had a real chance of winning."

Roland took another bite of turkey and bacon, chewed, and swallowed. "I see. How have relations between casters and shifters developed these last couple of months? I get the impression things are still frosty at best."

"Well, debatable," the other wizard extrapolated. "If anything, people are more pissed off at the Venatori. They're the ones who've broken the peace and fucked everything up. We haven't been legitimate *enemies* with the Weres for a while. There's the vague hostility of being different tribes, that sort of thing, but it hasn't gone beyond like when the fans of two rival sports teams see each other on the street or whatnot. Now, thanks to the Venatori, people—including witches—are getting killed. Then they have the *cojones* to try to militarize us and recruit us for their cause."

Roland nodded. It was making sense, and he could see the potential. He called for a drink refill, and his new friend ordered another too.

"So," Dante went on as they found themselves deep into their second beverage, "your relationship with Bailey is also kinda famous, and I have to ask." His eyes grew mischievous, and it was plain he was trying not to laugh. "Is it like banging a witch, or is it more like, um, a furry thing? Or would it qualify as bestiality?"

He broke off in snorting giggles at his own wit, then added, "Sorry, I joke."

"Silence," Roland replied in a theatrical voice, "and fuck off immediately." He wasn't being serious either, but if Bailey were present, he'd have had to advise the kid to watch it. "I have no idea how much action you get, even with all the raves and shit you seem to go to, but let's just say that most of the time, Bailey is a hell of a lot of woman. And I mean that in a good way."

"Fair enough," said Dante, suppressing his goofy smile.

Roland leaned back in his seat and his eyes went distant. "You know—and maybe you've heard about this—not long ago, I had three witches after me because they wanted to use me as a breeding stud. Don't ask me their names since I'd rather not divulge that information. Suffice to say that they were all hot as fuck."

The younger wizard stared at him. "*Seriously?*"

"Yeah." Roland sighed. "*Sounds* like a good deal, doesn't it? But you'd be amazed how quickly a woman's attractiveness stops mattering much when she's off her rocker and thinks you should be her goddamn slave. Three of them makes it that much worse. And it's not as though they gave a shit about *me.* They just wanted to climb the social ladder by having my children, since I was supposed to be this great magical prodigy and blah blah blah."

His head drooped toward his chest with the bitter memories.

"Oh, gosh," Dante shot back, his tone dripping with sarcasm. "Three hot girlfriends at once. Not *that.*"

Roland waved a hand. "Clearly you weren't paying any attention to what I said. Get yourself a sufficiently crazy girlfriend, and you'll find out. Not crazy as in 'different and interesting'—that's more like Bailey—but crazy as in 'should be institutionalized for the good of civilization.' Ugh, I don't want to talk about them."

"Well," Dante pointed out, "you're the one who raised the subject, but okay. Anyhow, I'm thinking we need to start by putting out a few anonymous messages on the boards, hiding our IP addresses as well as our magical signatures, to get a feel for who might be interested in helping us."

Before the black-clad wizard could go into more detail, a man in a suit and dark glasses strode into the bar. Roland recognized him immediately; it was the Agent who'd visited them at Gunney's shop and informed them of Townsend's situation.

Velasquez stood to the side of Dante. Looking down at the boy, his face was grim and humorless even by the standards of federal operatives.

"Please vacate the premises until I'm done talking to this individual," he stated.

Dante, despite his shy demeanor, flashed angry eyes at the intruder. The booze must have emboldened him. "The fuck? Who are you?"

Roland was about to suggest that Dante obey the man's reasonable suggestion when Velasquez produced as if by magic a tiny chrome pistol whose faintly glowing barrel was aimed straight at the wizard's face.

"This place," Velasquez mused, waving a hand around him. "Nice decor. Such high-quality windows. They look like they've just been washed. It would be a shame to splatter liquefied organic matter all over them. It would be difficult to clean off. You know what I mean?"

Roland nodded to his new friend. Dante swallowed, stood up, and trudged outside for the time being.

Velasquez sat down in his place. He waved the bartender away, and for her part, she seemed to recognize who he was—or who he worked for—and gave them a wide berth.

"Bad news," the agent intoned, getting straight to the point as his predecessor used to do. "Bailey's in danger. The Venatori are concentrating a huge force in the Northwest, and they're going to come after her personally while launching simultaneous strikes against vulnerable packs of Weres so she can't group everyone together and will come out with fewer living allies if she survives. We need to apprise her of the situation immediately."

Roland's nostrils flared. "Well, obviously."

Bailey's breath caught in her throat, partially in fear, but also in excitement. "There they are," she whispered.

Will and the other twenty wolves with her acknowledged her with slight nods. Most of them had already seen the witches, and the ones who hadn't were quickly brought up to speed. Crouching amidst the grass, bushes, and trees of their sacred ground, the lycanthropes were quieter and better-camouflaged than their intrusive opponents.

Of the approximately two dozen Venatori who'd penetrated into the Other, half were moving toward Bailey's forces. The other half were circling around the perimeter of the holy forest. The twelve they saw currently were further divided into two subgroups of six. Each half-dozen marched in a loose yet disciplined formation, and the two groups were only about a hundred feet apart.

Still, Bailey thought, *they should have kept their people together. One hundred feet is enough for us to get a wedge in and then divide and conquer their asses like we did to those legendary alpha spirits in the temple. We'll just have to hope they don't catch on and their friends don't suddenly show up.*

The ruse was working, though. Having initially drawn her aura-clones back to her after catching the sorceresses' attention, Bailey had dispatched them to move through the Other, their strong magical signature easily trackable by the eager invaders. The Venatori were clearly following the duplicates while ignoring the magical auras of Bailey and those of her alphas. In their lust to kill their main target, they apparently hadn't considered that the Weres might have duped them.

Granted, it helped that Bailey and Fenris had collaborated on a spell to muffle the arcane signature of her and her people. In the Other, *everything* was subtly charged with magic anyway. Thus, after the spell was cast, the members of the wolf pack were barely distinguishable from the supernaturally augmented trees and rocks.

The witches were almost upon them.

Concentrating hard, employing all the tricks she'd learned to break through the Other's magic-inhibiting barriers, Bailey sent out a psionic message to her troops: *Now.*

Rather than all attack at once, the only thing that happened was that two wolves burst out of the foliage and ran across a small glade slightly ahead of and to the right of where the Venatori were walking.

The half-dozen who were closer to the galloping Weres shouted something in French and moved off in pursuit of their quarry. The other group hesitated.

And the rest of the wolves pounced.

The Venatori had allowed themselves to be divided by

enough space for their attackers to cut them off from one another. Ten lycanthropes tackled each cluster of six, while Bailey sprang up and summoned thick, blinding-hot bolts of lightning to descend toward both groups. Half of them panicked and tried to run out of the way of both the lightning and the advancing Weres, and the rest were caught in the hopeless struggle of defending against magic versus defending against claw and fang.

Hairy forms piled into witches, and bodies rolled and tumbled. Snarls, screams, howls, and curses filled the air of the forest, which had been placid less than a minute before.

Bailey started with the half-dozen closer to her position. Her Weres had killed two of them, and only one had the elbow room to mount a magical counteroffensive. She flung out her hands to attack.

The werewitch struck her with a combination of shield and concussive energy at the very moment she cast her spell. The woman was knocked back while a storm of plasma blades got stuck in the arcane field, which Bailey forced back onto her, both crushing her to the ground and burning and stabbing her with her own fumbled spell.

As the witch died, her companions toppled under the wolves' onslaught. Some of the Weres were already bounding toward the other group of six, which was trying in vain to flee deeper into the woods.

Cruel exultation that frightened her rose in Bailey's chest. The witches were pushing deeper into her people's sacred land, and the wolves were on the verge of overtaking them. She ran after them to make sure she didn't lose any of her troops.

And ideally, to make sure the Venatori lost *all* of theirs.

She reached the edge of the new melee in time to mitigate the magical blasts the sorceresses sent toward her men. Two wolves went down yelping, dazed and injured but not yet dead. The others closed in from all directions, covered in part by the whirlwind of fire and ice Bailey conjured to disorient the witches and keep them pinned and on the defensive.

Soon enough, twelve motionless bodies lay strewn throughout the forest. The wounded on her side would live.

Bailey sent out another psionic call and drew the Weres back to her.

"We've cut their numbers in half," she announced as they assembled. Most were still in beast form, but a couple had shifted back. The two who'd taken blows were recovering off to the side, hidden amidst tall grass and wide trees. "Now there's only the other dozen to contend with. We've got two men down, but we can do it. Those of you who were with me in the temple, it'll be the same as when we took on the alpha spirits and the werebears. And I'll cover you with magic. Let's go!"

High on the adrenaline rush of victory and enthusiasm, the nineteen lycanthropes who could still fight assumed the form most natural to the woods and ran on all fours toward their adversaries. Bailey shifted too, assuming the new, smaller form she'd mastered to give herself more maneuverability.

Using magic in wolf form was a tad harder, but not much. When they caught the initial sights, sounds, and scents that led them toward the other twelve of the Venatori task force, Bailey had trouble imagining they'd fail.

The ghosts of their honored dead were watching over them here, and the holy forest would be the grave of those who'd violated it by their intrusion.

The first group of the remaining witches appeared on a ridge up ahead, their forms silhouetted against a curtain of leaves that glowed silver under the shining moon.

The wolves howled as one and attacked.

CHAPTER SEVEN

Roland didn't have a lot of confidence in his cell phone being able to reach Bailey under the current circumstances, but it was worth a shot.

"Come on," he breathed, speed-dialing her and waiting for the ringtone to resolve itself. Or not.

He stood in an alley not far from the bar and grill where he and Dante had been eating and drinking. The other wizard was lounging a couple of yards away, and so was Agent Velasquez. Shadows and garbage cans hid them from the main street.

The ringtone died before it had even started, followed by the automated message. "We're sorry, but the person you have dialed is not answering. Please—"

Cursing and gritting his teeth, he pressed End. "Not like I expected that would work." He waved a hand toward his companions. "Hold on, and I'll see if I can get hold of her the esoteric way."

He relaxed and let his eyes drift out of focus, his mind

expanding, consciousness rising and flying from him, expanding over the whole city and then seeking a path out of the world altogether. If indeed she was still in the Other, he *should* be able to track her magical signature within it and then mind-meld with her. It might not be possible to do so thoroughly enough to exchange coherent messages, but if nothing else, she'd realize he was trying to speak to her.

If it worked.

He recalled the techniques he'd used to open portals into the alternate dimension and modified them on the fly to admit astrally-projected consciousness rather than physical bodies. Part of his mind felt the familiar cold, dizzy sensation, followed by the damp and gloomy chill of the arcane realm.

Mere steps away from him, Velasquez looked at Dante. "You know what he's doing? Is this shit legitimately going to work, or are we wasting precious minutes?"

The kid shrugged. "I think he's trying to contact her via a psychic link. He's a more powerful wizard than I am, so I haven't been able to attempt anything like that before."

Velasquez grunted. There was only so much time to spare on failed attempts. They needed a foolproof method.

Roland's consciousness expanded throughout the Other, seeking familiar things. He detected the location of the dreaded Pool of Dark Reflections, as well as the sacred temple of the Weres within their enchanted forest. For an instant, he thought he found Bailey, but something was wrong.

Pulses of magical personality were running and ricocheting around, and nearly all of them seemed to be her.

His physical lips, back on Earth, mouthed the word, "How?"

He could not identify differences among or between them. It was as though she'd cloned herself, or multiple beings were disguised as her. And there were other things in the wolves' forest too, getting in the way. Shifting tides of magic and fury, expulsions of power, currents of emotion and thought. The entire area was becoming a chaotic mishmash of forces.

"No, dammit," he gasped and felt his grip on the Other slipping away from him. Fast enough to give him vertigo, his astral mind fell out of the arcane realm and rocketed back into his body. He experienced its return much like the sensation of crashing into the ground after a fall— shocking and painful.

Dante advanced toward him. "Shit. Are you okay, man?"

"Uh," he moaned, "yeah, just a sec. I'm fine. Or," he shook his head and fought down a wave of nausea, "I *will* be fine in a minute." He sucked in air and steadied himself.

Velasquez stepped up. "We don't have time to spare. If you can't contact her by magic, then you need to take us there in person. You can do that, can't you? We have to warn her, no matter what."

Roland blinked and dismissed the last of the disorientation. "I can, but we could end up in the wrong place. The Other isn't like Earth or any other planet in the universe as we know it. Both time and space are distorted, so it's tough to judge things like distance, area, or relative position. Even if I can get us to the place she seems to be, we might fall right into the middle of a gigantic clusterfuck. There was something going on in there. I'm worried the Venatori might have already found her."

The agent's fists trembled. "Shit! Is there anything you can do? I would have thought you'd be the man to go to, but it's starting to look like I should have asked my superiors instead and relied on Agency resources."

Frowning at the implied insult, Roland was about to snap at the man, but then a thought occurred to him.

"Actually, uh, yeah," he commented, "I just thought of something. It's—how should I put this—*atypical*, but I think it'll work."

"It had better," Velasquez warned.

Dante caught the other wizard's eye. "What do you have in mind? I might be able to help."

Roland shook his head. "Not with this. Well, maybe you can do auxiliary channeling. What I'm going to attempt is to summon Fenris. It might be our only chance."

The younger man's eyes widened in surprise. Velasquez betrayed no such alarm, but the way he tensed up suggested he appreciated the seriousness of such a notion.

"Fenris is *their* god, the patron of Weres. I'm on good terms with him, yes, but this could still bite me in the ass since you don't typically go around calling upon deities, and especially not ones that aren't your own. Bailey summoned Freya not long ago, and that was a massive risk. The gods tend to find stuff like that insulting. They're strange entities."

Velasquez shook his head slowly. "Gods. Never seen one, though from what Townsend told me, they're real enough. Do it, then. We don't have any other options."

Roland nodded, raised his arms, and closed his eyes. He

motioned with one hand for Dante to stand beside him, and the younger man started channeling arcane essence toward the other's position, feeding it to him for use in his endeavor.

Velasquez took three steps back. He'd easily surmised that it would be wise to stay out of the way.

Roland's voice rose like a wind. "O Fenris, wolf-father," he intoned, "wise and mighty lord of the forests that sprawl beneath the ever-shining moon. Hear me and heed my call. I, Roland, am one beloved to your favored daughter, Bailey. I have need of your knowledge. Move and appear. Manifest, for my cause is in line with yours. We seek to help and protect Bailey, and through her, the lycanthropic people. Fenris! Come forth!"

The god answered the call. Velasquez recoiled, struggling to maintain his composure. Dante blinked and stood frozen. Roland was only mildly surprised.

A beam of moonlight had descended from the clear daytime sky overhead, and where it struck the ground, silvery mist erupted in a swirling cloud. A black silhouette appeared within it, taking on the form and features of the large, hooded man whom Roland had once known as Marcus.

"Roland," the figure stated. "Why have you summoned me? I was watching over Bailey. She's drawn some of the Venatori into our sacred grounds within the Other to destroy them."

Velasquez took three steps forward, his steely confidence regained. "Hey, haven't I seen this guy before? You look familiar."

The deity cast a brief glance toward the agent. "Perhaps

you have seen me. Perhaps it was someone else. I can take different forms, after all." Then he looked back at the wizard.

Roland inhaled deeply. "Well, it sounds like Bailey's in trouble, but she's about to be in a bunch more. The Venatori are storming the beaches. Velasquez, do you wanna fill him in?"

The agent quickly summarized everything he'd previously told the wizard. Fenris' face, always solemn, grew graver still with the information.

Before responding, the deity looked at the younger of the two casters. "Who is this man? Do you trust him?"

Both Velasquez and Roland turned their eyes to Dante. Roland spoke up first.

"Yeah, so far. He wants to help us, and in fact was just talking to me about a recruitment drive to get more of the local witches on our side. I'd say we can use all the help we can get."

Velasquez chimed in with, "Agreed."

Fenris nodded. "Yes. And with the Venatori stepping up their attacks on the scale you speak of, our timetable is accelerated. We must intercept them directly and cannot afford to play games. The tactics we used last time will no longer suffice."

Dante listened, his face intent and his mind working to process all the new information.

As Fenris continued, his listeners grimaced. "Prior to and during the Order's last attempt, we were able to hop all around the continent, using the Other as a transit point from which to open portals and speedily rush to the aid of multiple communities. It worked because the Venatori's numbers were only sufficient to launch sneak attacks on small pockets of isolated rural Weres.

"But now," he went on, "they are attacking shifters within major cities, where the risks are greater, and storming entire towns of Weres with far greater forces. We cannot be everywhere at once. Also, with interspecies tensions reaching a boiling point, our intrusions might be misinterpreted as hostile movements against the witch community, as the Venatori tried to portray with their manipulated broadcast. No, we must draw the bulk of their forces into battle and try to defeat them on ground where we have the advantage."

Roland snapped his fingers. "Isn't that what you're doing?"

"Of course," Fenris confirmed, "though on a smaller scale. At this point, our best bet would be to pull every one of their units into the Other if possible and whittle away their numbers through hit-and-run tactics. If the Venatori concentrate on trying to kill Bailey and converge on her, we can bring in more Weres as reinforcements since with the witches no longer threatening pack-civilians in the mortal world, they won't need as much protection. We can focus all our available might on crushing them, perhaps once and for all."

Dante spoke up. "It's the same with witches who want the Venatori stopped." He sounded excited. "Part of the reason some of them don't want to get involved is because of the risk of reprisals against their families. But if the Venatori have practically *all* their available members fighting the main battle against Bailey, it would be easier to persuade them to join in."

Everyone concurred.

"Okay," Velasquez said, "but how do we make this brilliant plan happen?"

Fenris slowly raised his arms, and something in his eyes kept the others quiet as his thoughts seemed to coalesce. "Bait," he proclaimed. "Bailey, obviously, is the target they most want, and we have done much to draw them toward her. But it would help if I joined in the process."

"Uh," Roland pointed out, "didn't you say before that you weren't allowed to–"

The deity cut him off with a swipe of his hand. "Not openly, as Fenris. I shall pose as Bailey's right-hand shaman, her aide-de-camp and public face. I need only change my appearance, which is not difficult. And if I then proceed to make a great deal of magical noise, Aradia will notice."

Dante stiffened at the mention of the witch-goddess. The magnitude of the situation was dawning on him.

Fenris went on. "It may prove too tempting a prospect for Aradia to pass up. True, deities are not supposed to intervene in mortal conflicts, but she is already pushing the boundaries of what is acceptable. If our luck holds, she might slip into the Other since it's not considered part of the mortal world and attempt to quietly dispose of both Bailey and me together."

Velasquez's mouth twisted downward. "I hate to be the guy who asks the questions no one wants to hear, but what if she *succeeds?*"

"There's always a risk of that." The tall man shrugged. "But it would also be our opportunity to eliminate a dangerous rival god without enraging the rest of the divine pantheons. Not to mention wiping out the Venatori's military capabilities for two generations, leaving them broken and demoralized. Their leaders would lick their wounds and take time to contemplate the unwisdom of declaring war on my people."

Heavy silence settled over the dim alley.

Roland broke it with a clap of his hands. "Great! I love this idea. It's not like anyone has a better one. Let's fucking do this. But first, I could use a trip to the bathroom if that's okay."

Bailey pounced, a wedge-shaped arcane shield before her like the head of a battering ram. It divided and dispersed the blast of magical fire the grimacing witch before her threw toward her face.

Then the shield struck the woman, driving her into a tree, and Bailey dismissed it to leave the space before her jaws opened. She clamped them around the witch's throat and ripped it clear of the neckbone. A scream died in the ravaged windpipe, and the sorceress slumped to the earth.

The girl bounded up and took in the rest of the scene. Her wolves were winning, but one had been struck down with a plasma blade through the head, and others were taking light to moderate wounds. This time, the twelve witches had stuck together, and with the Weres' numbers reduced, they could not steamroll their opponents with the same ease as they had before.

Her heart briefly ached for the wolf who'd died. *I am all of you,* she thought, and that reminded her of the tactic she'd used against Madame Pataky in Greenhearth.

Leaping back into the fray, she jumped with magically-augmented speed, cloaked herself with invisibility so she winked in and out of sight, and never stayed in the same place for more than a split second. It created the illusion of an extra five or six werewolves joining the battle, and the witches' eyes flashed around madly, trying to take account of what was happening. Their morale was cracking, and the Weres swarmed over them.

Bailey shifted back into human form and caught one of the Venatori who tried to flee, tossing her into the air and then spearing her with a conjured icicle that pinned her to a thick silver trunk. The ice melted a moment later, and the corpse toppled back to the ground.

The noise ended and lungs heaved, desperate to refill themselves.

With the last of their enemies having fallen, Bailey shouted for her people to regroup and to bring the cadavers of the witches with them.

"Drag them this way," she instructed, "into the clearing between those two runestones. And don't mess them up any more than it took to kill them. We're gonna send a message, and being respectful with the bodies will send it all the clearer."

She supposed it was also her way of salving her conscience. She'd given into intense bloodlust during the engagement, eager to fight and kill, and a pang of guilt sounded somewhere beneath the surface sounds of her thoughts.

There were a few low growls at her command, and slight resentment simmered among the wolves. They all knew these women were trying to destroy them and Bailey most of all, yet they obeyed their shaman. Those who'd shifted back into human form carried the dead sorceresses over their shoulders. Those who were still in the shapes of beasts dragged them with their jaws over the grassy earth.

With the task done, one of the alphas turned to Bailey. "What do we do with them? Leave them here?"

The werewitch put her hands on her hips and looked at the grisly pile. "We'll bury them. I know it's our holy ground, but maybe that means that their spirits will mingle with the Were spirits around here and come to an understanding. But before we do that, everyone back off from this glade for a minute. I have an idea."

The wolves receded into the woods. Bailey stood in the middle of the laid-out corpses and recalled a spell Fenris had taught her perhaps a month ago. She'd had no cause to remember it until now.

It involved fixing a picture of a certain area in one's mind, then being aware of all the details and solidifying them into something like a magical snapshot. The image could then be sent to other people who were tapped into the arcane.

In this case, the Venatori leadership. Especially Aradia.

Bailey did the necessary mental work, checking the details around her, making the image as accurate as possible, and placing herself at its center, looking straight ahead with an expression of relaxed defiance.

The witch-goddess would see it, she knew, as she sent it toward the city of Lyon, France. The Order's ruling members would know that Bailey was right here, out in the open, standing before the bodies of twenty-four of their best, vanquished in their attempt to crush her.

And they would come.

CHAPTER EIGHT

Four men walked out of an alley and down the streets of Seattle. They moved with swift purpose but not to the point of outright haste. The tallest of them, who wore a bulky hooded coat despite the warmer weather, was the first to speak, although his words were drowned out by the noise of the city from more than a few feet away.

"I have surveyed the magical presences at work both in this region of our own world," he informed the group, "and in the Other. The Venatori are on the move, but it will be some time yet before the bulk of their forces are able to converge on Bailey. And they seem to be hesitating to strike at well-defended wolf packs."

Roland sighed with relief. "Finally, *good* news."

"As such," Fenris went on, "we should have time to implement our plans and refresh ourselves for the trials to come."

Agent Velasquez made a sharp grunting sound. "Good. We should probably part ways soon. I have another idea that I think could be highly effective."

Roland pursed his lips. "Do tell."

Velasquez turned his face toward Dante. "No offense, but I think you should get going. You've got other witches to recruit, don't you? And I don't know who the hell you are."

Dante blinked, obviously offended.

Fenris put a hand on the agent's shoulder. "He seems to be sincere. Still, Dante, it's true that you'd best get to work. And the fewer people who hear about a plan, the less likely it is that our foes will learn about it."

"Fine." The young wizard sighed. He waved goodbye and trudged off to the north, while the other three crossed the street to the west.

Once Dante was out of earshot, Velasquez resumed his spiel.

"As I was saying, I might be able to convince more of the Venatori to shuffle off into the Other after our girl. And I think they'd listen to me."

Roland gave him a cock-eyed look as though he'd spouted total gibberish. "You mean you're planning to, like, *talk* to them? Negotiate? Those are the people who went around from settlement to settlement, burning them down because they don't think Weres should be allowed to have magic."

"I know that," Velasquez snapped. "Hear me out. The Agency has had multiple violent encounters with the Venatori, enough to say we're officially at war with them. But sides fighting each other in a war *do* negotiate terms, especially when there's a change in personnel."

Roland suddenly felt a bit stupid, but he clamped down

on his tongue to keep himself from saying anything and waited for the agent to continue.

"Every altercation we've had with them," the man explained, "has ended with zero Venatori going back home. Not counting our double agent, of course. We either killed them all or took a handful of prisoners, all of whom we still have in custody. This means that they don't know what we're up to. Our facilities are well-protected against scrying and infiltration, so if there's reasonable cause to believe we're making a gesture toward them, they might well believe it."

Fenris rubbed his chin. "Yes, that makes sense. Go on."

"With Agent Townsend, who was pretty much supervising the whole conflict, being out for a long time and me filling his shoes, they might be receptive to the notion that we're adopting a change in policy. Therefore..."

Velasquez glanced around to ensure no one was too close or doing anything suspicious. There weren't many people on the street, and most who passed by took one look at the trio and walked faster to get clear of them.

"Therefore, I'm going to contact the Venatori and tell them where Bailey is."

Roland almost exploded with disbelief at that, but logical thought penetrated his emotions and kept him silent. *The Venatori have to go after her for our plans to work,* he reminded himself.

Fenris interjected, "They might suspect you're luring them into a trap."

"Maybe," Velasquez admitted. "But they know the Agency's prime directive is to keep things peaceful and quiet. Maintain the masquerade, you might say. That's been impossible lately. There's too much noise, violence, and chaos. I'll tell them I plan to stay out of the way and let them eliminate Bailey and her allies, provided they withdraw immediately thereafter and don't cause collateral damage. They'll believe me when I say that the shifters have gotten too powerful and are out of control. That's what they think anyway, so making it sound like I just want the dumb animals put back in their cages is playing into their presumptions and prejudices. We don't want the Agency's image tarnished. Witches blend in with the general population easier than Weres do. There's no reason to think they won't at least strongly consider the proposition."

"Hmm," Roland mumbled. "I don't *like* it, but you might be on to something there."

Velasquez adjusted his glasses. "No one likes the current situation. That's why we're trying to deal with it."

"Fair enough." Roland realized that Velasquez, who combined intelligence with a brusque demeanor, would probably do an excellent job of filling the void left by the unfortunate Townsend, at least in the short term.

Fenris gave a broad wave of his hand. "So be it, Agent. Implement your plan. It might contribute to their growing hubris and increase the likelihood that Aradia will get involved. But for the moment, we have a little extra time. I suggest we catch an hour's rest and perhaps a meal. It's difficult to say when we'll get another chance."

The two mortals readily agreed, although Velasquez seemed itchy to get to work. All three of them filed into the nearest greasy spoon, where they ordered strong coffee and Roland debated whether or not to get food.

"Dante and I just ate, like, an hour or two ago," he observed, "but as the big guy said, who knows what the future will bring? Might as well stock up on calories. I'm thinking nice, fattening comfort food, like mac n' cheese or a very large burrito."

"Knock yourself out," said Velasquez, "but not literally. Eating too much junk makes a person sluggish and inattentive. We don't want that."

The wizard frowned. "Okay, fine. I'll have, uh, chicken noodle soup then."

They drank their coffee and ate their early dinners. Fenris partook of the food, although he seemed somewhat ill at ease with it. Roland again found himself wondering if the humanoid deity took his regular meals in beast-form after hunting it himself in the woods.

The conversation turned to Bailey.

"She," Fenris stated, "is my biggest project in a long, long time. I have been waiting for many decades, if not centuries, for a werewolf of her caliber. She may be the leader our people have needed all this time, and she is the key to ensuring that our future is safeguarded."

Roland slurped his soup. "She's certainly a handful in more ways than one, and mostly good ways. It does seem like our lives completely revolve around her at any given millisecond, though. Most Weres, most women, most *people* can affect the course of events if they try, or not if they don't. With her, every movement she makes sends ripples across the proverbial pond."

Velasquez chuckled into his coffee cup, and his expression formed a sardonic grimace that was obvious despite the dark glasses covering part of his face.

"Townsend used to say that she was, uh, 'the Fifth Horseman of the Paperwork Apocalypse' or something like that. A walking shitstorm of fuckery he'd have to deal with."

"Well," Roland remarked, "that was nice of him." He frowned. "Still, it's too bad that he won't see the end of the conflict. He did a lot to help us, and now we—and Bailey—are going to win this war for him. If anyone can, it's her. With our help."

The agent nodded. "For all the disasters she causes, she's been even more of a disaster to the Venatori. Let's hope that trend continues."

"Oh," Fenris added, "I believe it will."

Former Grandmistress Gregorovia, together with Madame Dorleac and the other available members of the senior council, hustled into the ritual hall. Their goddess had called the meeting suddenly, and it was clear she expected no delay. There had been no time to make a formal and leisurely occasion of it.

The witches pushed through the doors and made for the throne before the altar at the rear, where Aradia sat. She was still and silent, yet powerful vibes of anger and prideful determination emanated off her earthly form like radiation from a warhead.

Gregorovia stopped before the throne, still standing, and caught her breath. "O great goddess," she inquired, "what do you desire of us?"

A gold-bedecked hand lifted into the air. "Look," Aradia commanded, her voice deceptive in its softness.

In the air before them, an image winked into sight. Like a hologram or strange airborne photograph, it showed Bailey Nordin standing over the corpses of Venatori operatives. Two dozen of them, including several prominent and talented witches, up-and-comers who'd been eager to hunt the werewitch down and blot her out at last.

"No!" Gregorovia cried. "How has she done this? Is she being aided by her god, as has been rumored? What tricks has she used to lay low so many of our brethren?"

Similar wrathful comments came from the other councilwomen, and their rage was genuine. They looked forward to the day Bailey's carcass would lie at their feet, yet they all made sure to display their antipathy as obviously as possible, so Aradia would see it and suspect no hesitancy or disloyalty on their part.

The goddess dismissed the image and looked at her followers. Her eyes blazed with fire.

"This," she hissed, the sound reverberating through the hall, "is your last chance to deal with the werewitch using your own limited powers. You may hold nothing further back."

The former Grandmistress swallowed, wondering if the goddess meant that even *they* should go after her.

"Aradia," she asked, "tell us how—"

"Your personal guards," the deity explained. "Your elite troops. The witches you have hoarded around your persons for the protection of your miserable lives. Are they not the best of your warriors? Send them. Send them at once! The woman you put in charge of the defense of this building and your Inquisitors. If *they* cannot destroy the girl, then our Order has failed, and *truly* extreme measures will be required."

Gregorovia swallowed and reflected on what her goddess had just demanded.

The Inquisitors were the cream of the crop, the last word in witchcraft. Taken as young children from among the most powerful casters of their generations, the Order groomed them as its ultimate enforcers. Indoctrinated from an impressionable age in the Venatori's ideology. Purged of pity and doubt. Taught all the ways of magic, of combat, of torture and interrogation, of spycraft —everything.

They served the senior council as a last line of defense and were also responsible for hunting down rogues and defectors from within the Order, not to mention unaffiliated witches who grossly offended their ideals. More than anyone else, the Inquisitors were the ones who gave the Venatori such a fearsome reputation in America and elsewhere.

Aradia had also insisted on sending Madame MacLachlan. She'd previously been a member of the senior council —the youngest in many decades, owing to her prodigious talent in battle—but Gregorovia had been forced to demote her to house guard after her failure to take Greenhearth.

"Yes," the former Grandmistress replied. "Of course. It shall be done at once."

Dispatching MacLachlan and the Inquisitors would leave the senior council and the Lyon headquarters virtually defenseless, aside from a small token contingent of middling troops.

"Good," Aradia echoed, and a deadly smile played on her lips. "Your very best fighters should suffice, should they not? I hope so for your sake. If they fail, I will hold both you and them responsible, for the Order itself will have failed. I will decimate this great institution that I raised myself in ancient times and rebuild it from the ground up."

Gregorovia went cold inside.

"But," the goddess added, "that shall be only my second order of business. If the Inquisitors fail, I shall first *win the war*. Myself. Regardless of any 'rules' that other beings have foolishly set."

Now the former Grandmistress felt sick to her stomach. Nauseous terror spread throughout the residual coven-mind of the councilwomen. If Aradia broke the covenant against divine intervention, the wrath of the other gods would destroy them all as surely as *she* would.

"That won't be necessary," Gregorovia insisted. "Our best troops will succeed. We will do whatever it takes. Preexisting information will allow us to hunt down Bailey Nordin and kill her at last, and if that proves difficult, the Inquisitors can easily apply pressure to the girl's family, friends, neighbors, even her lover."

Aradia raised her hands and the room darkened around them. "Do it. Do it all."

"Hah!" Madame MacLachlan grinned at her new companions. "I knew they'd rue the day they downgraded *my* status. If they'd done things the way I tried to do them to begin with, just wiping out all of the bloody brutes, we wouldn't be in this pickle, would we?"

The Inquisitors did not seem to share her enthusiasm, but it didn't bother her since they were taking their orders seriously. They took *everything* seriously.

MacLachlan could have been an Inquisitor, but she'd joined the Order two years too late. It had been enough time to grow a sense of humor, which had disqualified her from the position. She'd worked her way up to senior councilwoman in near-record time instead.

There were twenty-eight of them in the Chamber of Portals, nine Inquisitors, along with their eighteen assistants and the Scotswoman.

"I'm to be in charge of the Pacific Northwest expedition. Again," she reminded the others. "I know the lay of the land, having assaulted it last time I was there. Of course, since that's where Bailey and her dog pack are located, the bulk of you should come with me. Our mission is the most important of all."

One of the Inquisitors stepped forth. "Yes," she said in an icy monotone, "but you are to heed our advice in certain matters. That is an order from the Grandmistress. Understood?"

MacLachlan looked at the woman. Her name was Jarvis, and she had a long braid of black hair but was otherwise nondescript. Like the other members of her elite group, she wore leather the color of fresh charcoal, in contrast to the deep reddish hues favored by the regular Venatori.

"Fine," said the Scotswoman. "Try to make it *good* advice, then. Now, hop to it."

MacLachlan, Madame Jarvis, another junior Inquisitor

who hadn't divulged her name yet, and four assistant witches stepped through the portal that would take them to British Columbia.

After a moment of dizzying coldness, they emerged deep in the cellars of a shipping facility in Vancouver. From there, it was child's play to stow away on a boat and ensure it rapidly moved to Portland. Any officials who inspected the ship too closely were enchanted and mindwiped.

Mere hours after they'd left the hall in Lyon, the seven sorceresses had persuaded a car dealer to let them have a large-capacity van for free and without needing to do the necessary paperwork. They conjured a false license plate and drove it without delay toward the little town of Greenhearth.

"Do recall," MacLachlan told the others as they neared their destination, "that the lycanthropes have surrounded the entire bloody valley with volunteer patrols of their kind. Possibly some humans, too. We'd best stop well outside the town and have a look before we move in. Then again, the former Grandmistress *did* say that this was to be a terror mission, not a stealth one."

Madame Jarvis' mouth tightened. "We know this. Stop," she told her younger partner, who brought the van to a halt by a well-forested shoulder of the winding road.

They could all sense the presence of Weres nearby, the faint aura and the smell. Their mission would begin minutes after they stepped out of the vehicle.

All seven exited, alert and combative. MacLachlan was on the cusp of joy. She'd wanted a rematch with the wretched hamlet ever since she'd been kicked out of it. The

Inquisitorial personnel merely seemed focused on getting the job done.

They walked downhill on the side of the road, making no special effort to conceal themselves, and soon they heard the rustlings of rapid movement.

Dark, furry shapes burst out of the forest on either side of them. It was nothing they hadn't expected.

There were eight, maybe ten. MacLachlan, grinning fiercely, seized three of the human-sized wolves via telekinesis and hurled them hundreds of feet into the air, allowing them to arc naturally over a crevasse between wooded mountain peaks and then fall to their deaths within it.

Jarvis glared at the Scotswoman as she drove a Were back with a blast of icy wind. "At least one must live," she barked. "They must answer questions."

Though the lycanthropes fought to the limit of their abilities, the fight was over quickly. MacLachlan had to admit that Jarvis was her equal, maybe even her superior, in the field of arcane battle, with a particular talent for the manipulation of air and water. The wolves floundered, dead or unconscious, under the powerful assault, and soon only one remained.

"Hah!" MacLachlan scoffed. "Clearly your whole strategy was to hold the line until the Agency could ride to the rescue, was it? Your kind never were as hard as you thought you were."

Jarvis raised a hand, indicating the nominal leader should be silent, and stared into the wolf's eyes.

"Where is Bailey?" the witch asked.

The young man, for he had shifted back into human

form, his clothes half-torn near the armpits and knees, only growled at her.

Jarvis stepped in. Her hand shot out with blinding speed and dug into the man's armpit, making him spasm with pain as she forced him to his knees with inhuman strength. "Where is Bailey? Where is her *family?*"

MacLachlan snorted. "He's not going to talk, you know. We should just flatten the whole town and then pick the bodies of the Nordins out of the wreckage."

And indeed, the prisoner didn't. Jarvis encased his head in a sphere of water, pushing him to the brink of drowning before dismissing it, but still he said nothing. He was prepared to die in defense of his loyalty oath.

Jarvis' eyes narrowed. "Very well. We shall make an example of you."

Four more Weres ran up the street toward the group, from the town proper, snarling, and half-shifting as they moved. With an offhand motion Jarvis cast a lateral blade of wind at them, cutting all four in half at the waist or chest. Then she looked back at the captive.

"I have an idea," MacLachlan proposed. "Let's leave him here. For a long, long time."

She twisted her fingers, and the werewolf levitated into the air. He could barely flail his limbs, as though underwater, but he did not move to the side, only straight upward. His ascent stopped about seventy meters from the ground. At the present altitude, he'd stand out in the sky, readily visible to anyone in town who looked.

MacLachlan wove long-lasting strings of basic magic to tie the wolf in place.

"There," she stated. "The spell will last long enough for

him to die of hunger, thirst, exposure, and the like. No one will be able to save him or bring him down. I'll stand guard over him and do unpleasant things to him until further notice. Nothing fatal. Low-level electric shocks, shallow lacerations, perhaps telekinetic kicks and punches to the groin. We can relieve him when the townsfolk begin to cooperate. *Which they will.*"

Jarvis nodded. "Yes. Come, let us search the town and question those people."

As they set off into Greenhearth, the Inquisitor reminded her subjects of the necessary procedure. "No resistance is to be tolerated. It must be dealt with immediately and *harshly.*"

CHAPTER NINE

With Agent Velasquez having left to implement his devious ploy, Roland got back in touch with Dante, composing a text message to him near the corner of an empty lot while Fenris watched over his shoulder.

Before the wizard could send the message, he was interrupted by an incoming call. His phone recognized it as the number from Gunney's auto shop.

"What the heck?" he remarked. He swiped his finger across the screen. "Hello? Gunney?"

"Roland," the mechanic's voice sounded, and there was a harsh note of fear in it that made the wizard's abdomen clench up. "We got major trouble back on the home front. Every damn Were in town is in danger, and probably most of the humans besides. The Venatori are back, but instead of an army, this time, it's a small group of hell, super-witches. Two of them are in black leather instead of that usual maroon or whatever, and I'm pretty sure another is the bitch who commanded that big assault about a month ago. They killed at least a dozen wolves so far, and they've got one poor schmuck—Doug, I think—suspended in midair and being tortured."

The wizard closed his eyes and ran a hand through his hair. "Oh, hell. What do they want? Bailey?"

"Yeah," Gunney responded. "They've been kicking down doors and brushing aside anyone who tries to fuck with 'em. I've never seen witches as powerful as these ones. No one can lay a finger on them. They keep asking where Bailey is, but we don't have the slightest idea! And they want to know where her brothers are, too. I'm not sure of that myself. I thought they knew where the Nordin house was, but they'll find them soon, I'm sure. And for all that those three are tough bastards, I don't think they can handle these ladies by themselves."

Fenris, listening in, started to speak, but Roland was way ahead of him. "Tell them that Bailey's in the Other," he said, his words almost spilling over each other, "but she never said exactly where she was going. Which is the truth, anyway. We're trying to get them to come after Bailey into the Other. No collateral damage that way. Find them and tell them."

"It ain't gonna be that simple," Gunney sighed. "They're trying to lure Bailey out so they can dogpile her on their own terms. Based on what they're doing to Doug, I'd guess the idea is to force her hand by threatening her family. With your help, maybe they could overpower them. But then you'd be at risk too. These witches are nothing to fuck around with, Roland. No offense, but I'm not sure even you could deal with them."

Inquisitors, Roland thought. *I thought they were just an urban legend, or the Venatori had already sent them in normal uniforms. I guess not. We're finally getting to deal with the creme de la creme.*

Gunney went on. "I can't get hold of Bailey if she's in a damn alternate dimension. You and Fenris might be the only ones who can help. I could try that agent's number, but you never know with those people."

"We're on it," Roland replied. "If they question you, again, tell the truth. Try to stall them, but don't put yourself in unnecessary danger. Them going through a portal into the Other is part of the plan, anyway, and at least it'll mean Greenhearth is safe. But we're coming. Hang tight."

The older man's voice came in a wheeze. "I hope you're right. So long."

Roland hung up. "You heard that, obviously," he said, turning to Fenris. "What the goddamn hell do we do now? Me trying to fight that caliber of witchcraft would be a coin-flip at best, and I'm guessing you're still not going to help out."

The god's face was stony, but subtle tremors of wrath were going through his body. "I cannot intervene directly. You know this. But I will help however I can. Message your friend and gather any volunteers you can—wolves, witches, or anyone willing to help. Then I can open a portal to take you to the Hearth Valley. From there, it will be up to you."

"Yeah," was Roland's only comment. He finished composing his text and shot it off to Dante, resolving to call the kid if he didn't reply post-haste.

Fortunately, it only took a minute or so. The response indicated Dante had had some luck convincing two witches to help out, and he might convince a third with more work. That was far fewer than Roland would have liked, but it sounded like they were powerful casters.

Fenris inhaled. "Tell him to keep working on the third witch, and bring any others he can. You, meanwhile, should see to your contacts, including the local Weres you spoke to earlier. We can spare perhaps one hour while the townspeople stall the Venatori. Then we must move."

"Agreed." Roland sent the next text, then asked the tall shaman if he could open a portal within Seattle to get him to the Holmquist residence.

Fenris grimaced. "I am pushing the limits of what is allowed," he observed, "but then, so is Aradia. We have no choice but to respond to her aggression and manipulation in kind." He raised his arms, uttered a chant, and opened the portal.

"Thanks," Roland said and stepped through into the Other. From their usual transit-point in the arcane bog, Fenris opened another doorway that led straight to the Were family's backyard. The wizard just hoped that no normies had seen him step out of a glowing gateway in midair.

The backdoor opened, and Mrs. Holmquist looked at him in dull shock.

"Hi!" He waved. "You remember me, right? Well, I meant to come to the door again, but I was in a slight hurry. So anyway, Bailey's in trouble, and I was wondering if I could ask for your help with something."

Nine figures stood amidst the fog that swirled around the boggy ground while the black claws of dead trees reached toward a clouded-over sky of deep purple. Facing the rest of the group was Fenris.

"Are you all in agreement?" he asked the other eight. "Are you prepared for what's to come? If so, I will open the gateway to the auto shop, so that you can reconnoiter with Gunney before engaging the Venatori."

Roland and Dante stood at the head of the octet. They looked back at their new allies to gauge their reactions.

Each wizard had drummed up three volunteers. The quantity might be lacking, but the quality was not.

Dante had succeeded in convincing the third witch he'd mentioned to join them. All three were women, which was a good sign, given the usual gender imbalance in magical talent among their species. Slender goth types mostly, although the one—Charlene, if Roland remembered right? —was wearing a blue shirt instead of black.

Meanwhile, Roland had gotten Mr. Holmquist and two of the late Greg Holmquist's friends to tag along for a little payback against the organization that had introduced them to tragedy. The older gentleman was at least fifty, and perhaps not as fast as he'd once been, but he was still powerful and claimed to have learned a few fighting tricks over the decades that more than made up for his decreased agility. The younger Weres were named Jon and Trevor. Jon had left the club where Greg had died only ten minutes prior to the arrival of the Venatori's hit squad. He seemed consumed with survivor's guilt.

"Well," Roland had told him, "now's your chance to vent

some of that negativity on the people who most have it coming."

The two trios mostly clustered among their own kind. They were willing to work together, but it appeared they expected Roland and Dante to lead them separately as sub-groups within the overall force.

But with all eight about to head back to Greenhearth, they would have to do whatever was necessary.

Roland spoke for them all. "We're ready. We haven't had a lot of time, but we discussed general tactics, and we all want to do this."

Nods and grunts of assents went around the octet.

Fenris turned away from them. "So be it." He chanted the words that would open the necessary portal.

To defuse the tension, Roland said to Dante's recruits, "It's nice to see some ladies in the party. That ought to maximize our firepower."

"Thanks," Charlene replied curtly.

Dante squinted in confusion and nudged at the other wizard. "I thought you were supposed to be, like, the exceptionally powerful one."

Roland rubbed one of his eyes. "I am, *for a male.* Chicks are generally stronger than dudes when it comes to magic, which puts me in the upper-middle range of casters over-all. I mean, I'm no slouch, but frankly, I'm not a match for the top-tier female witches."

"Oh," Dante muttered. "Right. Damn."

"It is what it is." Roland shrugged.

Fenris had conjured up the gate, and he swiped a broad hand before their faces. "You have enough concentrated power between you all—both arcane talent, and the more primal strength of shifters—to confront even the Venatori's elite. And you know the importance of our cause. Go to it and make swift work of them, because time is short. Soon you will face no mortal caster, but a goddess. Then we'll need the help of *everyone*. No one's life or contribution will be superfluous."

Roland whistled. "Melodramatic but true. Off we go, folks." He led the way and practically skipped through the portal, sensing rather than seeing Dante and the others piling in behind him.

The icy disorientation lasted only a second, then he emerged onto a dusty open space hemmed in by low hills and trees. Fenris had chosen the site of the doorway's other end perfectly. They were in the backlot of Gunney's shop, hidden from the view of anyone on the street, but able to see around them right away. No one was nearby.

On the downside, that put them far across town from Doug. Roland could barely see the unfortunate lycanthrope hanging in midair over a side road leading into the hills to the west.

Roland figured he was the leader of the group if anyone was. He turned to address them.

"Okay, let's head into that shop, being quiet and inconspicuous about it. The guy who runs the place is the one who asked me to come help, so it's not like he'll object, but we don't want to make a lot of noise. We don't know where the Venatori are yet."

With that, he crept toward the rear office door. His seven companions followed. The repair bays were all closed. Gunney must have shuttered the shop once the Venatori rolled into town.

Roland knocked on the glass. Within was Gunney, who looked surprised and nervous for a second. He got over it once he recognized the wizard. The stubby old man cleared the floor in three long strides and pulled it open.

"Nice to see you, Roland," he greeted him. "Too bad about the circumstances. Who are these folks?"

Roland quickly introduced them. "Seattle's finest. A nice mixture of Weres and witches. All people who know what they're doing in a fight, too."

"Well, good," the mechanic grumbled, flipping his cap off his greasy mop of hair before pulling it back down. "I worry that you might not have enough to take them all on at once, but that's where the good news comes in. There's only seven of them, and they've split into two groups to cover more of the town at speed, not counting the one who's hanging around and beating up poor Doug. That means two groups of three. Each one consists of one of the black-suited ones and two in regular uniform. Not very many, but those ladies in black are freakishly powerful. Like nothing I've seen before."

Murmurs of concern went around the group.

Roland spoke to everyone at once. "Trickery and the element of surprise have a way of neutralizing raw power," he pointed out. "So we've got a chance. Gunney, what are they doing right now? And where are they?"

The mechanic explained that the witches were going door-to-door, demanding to know where Bailey's family was. One group had started at the Nordin house, but the brothers must have vacated it or were simply somewhere else in the valley since the witches were still searching.

"They've been at it for a good hour," Gunney explained.

"Probably been through half the town. Either they'll find the Nordin boys and do God-knows-what to them, or they'll find nothing and then probably retaliate against the whole damn town. They wiped out the outer patrols in the west. Not sure what they did with the other guard-Weres or Sheriff Browne and his deputies, but it can't be good. Trapped them in buildings at best, imprisoned with magic. At worst..."

His voice trailed off into silence.

Roland's jaw muscles tightened. "We need to stop them before they finish their sweep. First thing is, we need to stick together. Eight of us versus three of them, freakishly strong or no, is decent odds, but against all six or seven at once, not so much."

Everyone agreed to that. Then Dante chimed in with another idea.

"They're from Europe, right?" he began. "They haven't met any of us besides Roland and Bailey and maybe a few people in town if any of them are the same witches who attacked before. Those of us from Seattle are unknowns. It's not like we were major players in the witchcraft sphere anyway."

Gunney squinted. "So, you're saying to sneak up on them?"

"No," the young wizard clarified, "I'm saying go up and talk to them. We can pretend to be locals since they won't know the difference. Say we've lived here alongside the Weres the whole time, and are getting sick of how lycanthropic problems are threatening everyone else, and we've decided to rat them out and be done with it."

"Ah," Roland murmured. "And lure them into a snare. Nice."

Dante smiled. "Yeah, basically. Bring one of the two groups of three back here so we can jump them and halve their numbers before they have the chance to sound the alarm."

Charlene interrupted. "Wait. What if they insist on gathering the other group before they come back?"

"Shit." Dante hung his head.

Roland shook his head. "Unless anyone else has a brighter idea, I say we go with Dante's. It'll probably work if we can catch one of the groups when they're close to the shop. They might get overexcited and not think of regrouping before they move in for the kill."

Some of the faces before him looked hesitant, but no one objected or came up with anything else they could do instead.

Mr. Holmquist shrugged his broad shoulders. "Let's do it. I'll be out in front when we ambush them. I don't want to go home until I've killed at least one of them. My boy never did a single damn thing to them. He was just in the wrong place at the wrong time."

One of his late son's friends put a hand on his arm, and Roland gave them a moment before he spurred them on. "Okay, good. We're committed now. Quick huddle on the specifics, then we make it happen."

Five minutes later, Dante led his trio of female volunteers out of the body shop after Gunney opened the central repair bay door. The Seattle witches tried to keep out of sight at first, but once on the main street, marched boldly down its center. The town was deathly quiet around them.

Roland watched them go. There was no telling how long they'd be gone, so he took the opportunity to get better acquainted with his new companions.

"It's strange," the wizard mused. "I grew up in Seattle, but I never interacted with Weres aside from once in a great while, and then it was only polite interaction at parties or businesses or whatever. But here I am living in a town full of shifters, and I know *them* better than I ever got to know you guys. Maybe we can make up for lost time."

Mr. Holmquist was still tense from thinking about his son, but he grasped that Roland was trying to make conversation. "Yes, we always kept to ourselves as well. Too many misunderstandings can turn up between different species, especially when both of us have to pretend to be human half the time. That's one thing we have in common."

"No shit," Jon added. "I always figured Weres and witches were on the opposite sides of humanity, though. Like, we're off to their left toward the woods at night, and you guys are off to their right toward the crystal spires and civilized intellectual stuff."

Roland's eyes went distant as he contemplated the analogy. "That's an interesting way of putting it. I think it's more complicated than that, but not bad."

Trevor added his two cents. "Well, this whole mess is teaching me that we've got more in common than different. I think."

Gunney asked them, "You guys want something to eat or drink? There's stuff in the shop fridge over there in the corner. That's one thing we all got in common, for sure."

Roland had eaten two meals within two hours previously, so he declined, but the three wolves raided the fridge, coming back with a nice deli tray and bottles of soda. The wizard noted with relief that they'd all gone for cola or lemon-lime, meaning there'd still be orange waiting for Bailey when she got back.

The mechanic weighed in as his guests tried to relax. "Shit," he grumbled. "Normally I'm not one to worry too much—Lord knows I've advised Bailey to lighten up enough times—but I gotta confess, things are looking worse than ever. This shit today is downright scary. Last couple times the Venatori came here, there were big battles, which was bad enough in a way, but today? Nothing. What are they doing out there? Do they have so much magical talent that six of them can pacify the whole town while they probe through every goddamn house?"

His anxiety was contagious. Roland decided to cure it immediately.

"I don't think so," he said. "They're probably being stealthy and careful, is all. The last two times were military invasions, after all. This is more like a black op. There *are* spells that will put people to sleep, hold them in place, make it impossible for them to scream, or use a phone— stuff like that. But there's no reason to believe that they've killed everyone who might resist them if that's what you're thinking. Now *we're* going to be the ones ambushing *them.*"

Saying that, he felt better at once, and half the misgivings melted away from the three Weres, too.

Gunney shook his head. "I hope you're right. You're a smart kid, but I'd feel better if Bailey were here."

"Me too," Roland confessed. "She's already dealt with stuff worse than this. But the reason she isn't here is that she's raising an army to deal with the problem at its source. All we have to do is get rid of half a dozen witches. We got this."

Silence set in, but it was now less marred by nervousness.

Moments later, figures appeared at the mouth of the side road that led up from Main Street toward the shop. Glimpsing them through the front windows, Roland strained to see, hoping Jon's and Trevor's eyesight was better than his.

It appeared to be seven people total. If so, that meant Dante had succeeded thus far. He still had his three followers, and they'd pulled one of the Venatori trios away from the other. But he couldn't make out their faces yet.

The wizard looked at the lycanthropes. "Can you guys see who it is?"

Jon sprang up. "It's Dante, all right. And there are three women behind him in weird leather catsuits. One in black, two in kind of a reddish-brown or dark purple, I think."

Roland nodded and took a deep breath. "That's them. Everyone, get in position. Gunney, in your case, that means getting the hell out of the way and staying somewhere safe. Maybe behind the dumpster out back."

The mechanic waffled. "Just behind the *building* for now, we'll say. Good luck!"

Roland stood in the repair bay, not too obviously in plain sight but making no effort to hide, either. Mr. Holmquist stood nearby, and they pretended to talk. Jon and Trevor had taken up positions in the dark corners to either side.

Dante stormed toward the shop. "They're here!" he

cried, pointing. "That's her boyfriend, and that guy is her *dad!* Hurry before they run away!"

The young wizard stepped off to the side, then, and his three female companions hung back, staying in the rear as the Venatori advanced.

Roland looked toward the lot and pretended to be frozen in shock. Holmquist threw up his arms in despairing rage. He probably had plenty of that particular emotion to draw upon for his act.

"Dante!" he roared. "How could you! We've been neighbors for twenty-five years, man. I trusted you!"

The Venatori came closer. Their sable-clad leader, a slim witch with short auburn hair, said, "Dante has done what he should have. He will be rewarded with a place among us where he belongs if he chooses, and some of our members may reward him in other ways, too. Nothing is too good for him who turns against the werewitch."

To her sides, the assistant sorceresses smirked, and one flashed Dante a wicked eye-batting glance. The boy swallowed.

"And," the Inquisitor added as she stepped over the threshold of the shop, "we have found the traitor wizard. Our work here will be done very soon."

"Exactly right, bitch!" one of Dante's recruits screamed. Then all hell broke loose.

Lightning and fire blazed through the air, shields crackled into existence and then dissipated, winds howled, and Weres shifted and pounced. Roland focused on trying to neutralize the Venatori's magic, surrounding the Inquisitor with layers of shields and waves of psionic force.

Anything to occupy her while the others picked off her assistants.

For all the black-clad leader's power, the ambush had been too well-executed. Holmquist and Jon ripped the left-hand assistant to shreds while Dante, Charlene, and the others blasted the right-hand one with flame and then tossed her head-first into the metal door rack.

The Inquisitor's eyes burned with hateful rage, but she kept her composure, and in the seconds that stretched across the battle, she began to inexorably quash Roland's magical efforts. But she was surrounded, and after her henchwomen fell, five other casters and three Weres assailed her at once.

Jon and one of the Seattle girls toppled back with sudden burns on their limbs, and everyone reeled under the rising wind, but it wasn't enough. Holmquist bit the woman's leg, and Roland tossed a plasma lance through her face that came out the back of her skull before it dissolved in a wisp of smoke. She fell, landing on the pavement with a thud.

Quiet set in as Roland dashed over to check on the wounded. They'd taken nasty scorches and would at the very least need them bandaged and anesthetized, but they'd live. Still, he debated calling an ambulance.

Gunney came back in from the rear.

"God-fucking-dammit," he cussed, smacking a rag against the wall. "How the hell am I supposed to clean this mess up? We're lucky there wasn't a customer's car in the middle of all that blood. This place is set up to handle oil spills, gas leaks, and service fluids, not fuckin' *bodily* fluids."

Agent Velasquez cheered in his mind as the video call finally patched through, though he kept his face stony and imposing behind his black sunglasses. Behind him was only a black wall.

The picture flickered into clarity, showing a middle-aged woman frowning at him severely. The nondescript decor around her looked like something out of a normal, modern office building. Velasquez was disappointed. He'd hoped the witches would have addressed him from a decaying castle.

"Who are you?" she demanded in a French accent. "How were you able to contact us?"

"Aw," Velasquez shot back, "it's cute that you thought I *couldn't* contact you. Well, I did. We have our ways. And even if you don't know who I am, individually, I think you know who I'm speaking on behalf of."

The witch's frown deepened. "Yes. What do you want?"

"There's something you ladies need to be aware of," the agent stated. "Let me speak to whoever is in charge. The higher their rank, the better. It's extremely important."

The woman looked aside, presumably seeking feedback from another person who was out of visual range, then visibly snorted at the camera. "No. We have nothing to discuss with you."

"*Hold on*," Velasquez barked, his voice loud and sharp, and he raised a fist beside his face. "It's about the growing shifter problem. You know that the Agency is responsible for keeping all supernatural beings in line in America. And lately, the biggest problem is the goddamn werewolves."

The witch seemed to consider his words. Again she glanced to her right, and an unspoken message passed between her and whoever else was present. Over a minute went by, and Velasquez assumed that an entire conversation must have been occurring via psychic methods.

At last, the scowling woman turned her eyes back toward him. "You have fought us just as fiercely as the lycanthropes have, and suddenly, you are our friends? Hah!"

Velasquez pushed his glasses up his nose with one finger and sighed with what he hoped was exactly the right mixture of tiredness, exasperation, and cynical opportunism. "Yeah, sorry. I was too low-ranking to have any effect on the decision-making process until recently. After Townsend got injured, I took over his position until he gets back—if he ever does. Looks pretty bad for him. And now that I *do* have authority, I'm telling you that I intend to drop Townsend's personal vendetta against the Order and focus on fulfilling our Agency's primary mission. *Keeping the peace.*"

Once more, the silent conference between two or more witches. Then the one in front of the camera said, "We are listening. But do not assume we have forgotten your recent actions."

"Right, right," he drawled, trying to convey the sense that he'd been merely doing his job and was tired of it. "The Agency's foremost concern is preventing conflicts between paranormal entities from affecting the outside world of normal humans. That has become impossible, and a major part of that is the growing power and militancy of werewolves, see? Bailey and her closest followers can no longer be controlled, and we want something done about that. We *don't* want an all-out war, so it has to be done quietly. But the Agency is willing to turn a blind eye to any actions taken against the Nordin girl at this point."

The witch's face scrunched with annoyance. "What do you think we are trying to do?"

Velasquez let a sly smile creep across his face. "I can tell you exactly where she is," he offered. "But only if you will let me speak to the leader of the Order. I want to deal with her directly."

The woman turned and left the picture. There were a couple of minutes of silence interspersed with faint shuffling, then a handsome elderly woman with a deep burgundy hood drawn over her silver hair came into the picture.

"Good day," she opened with a curious accent, possibly a blend of French and Italian. "I am Grandmistress Gregorovia, the head of the Order. My assistants have relayed all you said to them. Please tell me where we can find the girl, and we will agree to your terms."

Velasquez inclined his head. "Good day back to you, Madame. With all due respect, though, I said the *leader*. We are aware that you're no longer the one in direct control."

The woman's eyes flashed with indignation, but she calmed down quickly enough, then said, "So be it. But I am not responsible for how much you *enjoy* speaking to *her*. Wait, please."

Well, Velasquez thought, *this ought to be interesting. I get to meet my second deity in two days!*

The screen went dark. The image crackled and shifted, like an old TV set that needed its antenna adjusted, and the device's internal cooling fan went into overdrive. Velasquez hovered his hand over it, suddenly afraid the damn thing was going to overheat.

Then it ended and the picture returned, brightening by gradual measures back to normal lighting. In the center of the screen, surrounded by walls of ancient stone, was a tall, stunning woman with well-coiffed black hair and flowing robes of the same color, bedecked with golden finery. Her shining eyes seemed to stare through the screen, and Velasquez felt cold, nearly sick, from looking into them. For all that the figure was beautiful, she radiated an aura of watchful primordial menace.

"I," she stated, and the screen vibrated in time with her voice, "am Aradia, the first lady of witchcraft. And you are a mortal man who has requested an audience with me. What do you hope to achieve by so doing?"

The agent pushed aside his fears. "Yeah, very tough facade you have there, ma'am, but I'm aware of the universal pact against deities acting directly against us mortals, so I know you're in no position to harm me."

The goddess' expression did not change, but her eyes bored more deeply into him, the sensation both too cold and too hot. He forced himself not to shudder.

"I have an offer for you," he went on. "As I told your servants, we of the Agency want this whole mess with the werewitch and her little personal army cleared up. They're making a huge mess. So, if you'd be interested, we can tell you where she and her closest followers are, and how to find them. It's in a place where no one would notice anything untoward—including small technical violations of the divine non-intervention pact. My organization will stand by, do nothing, and say nothing as long as you take care of it *quietly.*"

The haughty lips within the aristocratic face drew upward at the corners. "I am intrigued. Somehow I had suspected that you people were as self-serving as the rumors suggested. We have no wish to destroy the world, only to allow my daughters to flourish within it, which cannot occur so long as Bailey makes war on us."

"Right," Velasquez shot back instantly. There was no point in pretending he *believed* the Venatori's self-serving justification for their crusade. If anything, seeming cynical and indifferent enforced the idea that he was playing both sides against the middle to cover the Agency's collective ass.

"Tell me," Aradia insisted, "and it shall be done without public spectacle."

The agent cracked his neck and readjusted his glasses. "Okay. But a couple more conditions if you don't want my colleagues making life difficult for your daughters. First, you need to stop all those random attacks on American shifters. Without Bailey and her top shamans and friends, the rest of them will settle back into being mostly harmless. So leave them alone once she's dealt with."

"Done," said Aradia. "What is the other condition?"

"Second," Velasquez added, "you must make absolutely certain she's dead. That means bringing whatever power to bear you think is necessary. The girl is tough. She's survived multiple attempts by powerful Venatori to kill her. Hell, since she's somewhere beyond human perception anyway, you could take care of her yourself. In fact, that might be the best way. She's strong, but she can't defeat a goddess."

The woman's smile widened. "Done. She *will* die, no matter the cost. I will uphold your terms, provided you uphold yours. If you betray us, we will crush your Agency as surely as we are crushing the lycanthropes. Now, tell me where the werewitch may be found!"

It occurred to Velasquez that Aradia's threat was not an empty one. The Agency was formidable, but a prolonged war with the Venatori when they were backed up by their new goddess might be unwinnable. If the ploy failed, things would become far worse than they already were.

He cleared his throat. "So, then. She's in the Other near the werewolves' temple, in this sacred forest they have. I think they were trying to meditate in the presence of the ancient shamanic spirits before the big battle or something like that. She's got a few Weres with her, including a couple of shamans, I think, but nothing your heavy hitters can't deal with. She's separated from the rest of her people, and there will be no witnesses or human casualties."

The deity's eyes blazed in a way Velasquez could barely look at them. "Good," Aradia stated. "I know of the region you describe. My elite forces will strike her directly, and then I shall follow."

The screen went black after crackling loudly. Velasquez sat blinking at it before he noticed that a wisp of smoke was rising from the device.

"Shit!" he exclaimed. The thing was dead. It was not meant to receive transmissions from entities who gave off levels of power comparable to the sun. "One *more* thing that will require me to fill out twenty goddamn forms."

He went to the bathroom and splashed cold water on his face. Staring into the mirror, he wondered if he'd done the right thing.

They were putting Bailey in severe danger. There was no guarantee the crazy plan to assassinate the goddess would work, and if it didn't, Aradia would make the other pantheons aware. It might be just as bad as if Fenris had started laying waste to witches himself.

"It's our only viable option." He sighed. "Fuck. Now I see why most days, Townsend hated the job so frickin' much."

CHAPTER TEN

"I can't believe we're having a damn *picnic*," one of the lieutenants said. His tone was gruff, but his broad, bearded face was softened by a warm and goofy smile. He was a Silver Star named Don, Roger's replacement right-hand man since Jim had been killed at the nightclub.

Bailey shrugged. "Who knows when we'll get another chance? I haven't had a picnic in quite some time. Seems nice."

Half the other wolves chortled, including Roger, who pretended to admonish his man. "Shut up, Don. You're just mad that we only brought enough food for one meal instead of eating two or three at once."

"Hey," Don protested as the other Weres laughed, "most of my pounds are pure muscle."

"Yeah," someone said, "I used to hang out with this really fat kid who always told me the same thing."

Bailey raised a hand. "Come on, now, don't get nasty. I think we're all hungry enough to eat two meals at once for the time being."

It was true. Despite the way the Other suspended the needs of the body, intense battle plus the exertion of burying two dozen bodies had famished them.

Must be a mental hunger, Bailey reflected. *We all think and feel that we're supposed to be hungry at a time like this. But it's not only that. The ugliness of killing all those women, and the danger we're in? It's made everyone want to have a proper, civilized, sit-down meal. Like friends and neighbors. Human beings.*

That would also explain why they made their dinner from supplies the Weres had brought. There was ample game in the enchanted wood, which any of them might have hunted with ease while shifted into wolf form. Bailey had forgotten to tell the newer guys they didn't need to bring food into the Other.

She was glad they had, though. They shared sandwiches and sodas from coolers and opened bags of chips and trail mix. Bailey absentmindedly thought she could use a beer, but drinking at a time like this was unlikely to be wise.

More Weres had shown up after the initial battle was over. Bailey sent a couple of them back, taking the wounded with them to get help, but welcomed the addition of the others. Their numbers had swelled to at least three dozen. Some had never met each other before.

Conversation turned to a review of all they'd been through—especially her and those who'd been with her previously, not least Will, Roger, and the others of the South Cliff and Silver Star packs who had gone through the temple's trials together.

"Shit," Bailey said, "I remember when half of you thought I was a loose cannon coming to take over your packs. And here we are, friends."

Alfred Warner, the aging but still formidable shaman of the Whitcomb Creek pack down by Salem, had emerged from the crowd and was munching a bag of nuts, seeds, and dried fruit.

"Yes, I recall," he commented. "I'm glad we cleared up that misunderstanding quickly. Well, you *have* taken over, but it's for the best. We need an exceptional leader in a time like this. Who could have anticipated the Venatori would declare war?"

Will Waldsbach shook his head and bit into a salami sandwich. "It's crazy," he remarked through a mouthful of food. "It was only a couple of months ago that the South Cliffs were still run by Dan Oberlin, who either wanted to marry Bailey or kill her or maybe both. He turned out to be even more of an asshole than anyone thought. Now he's in jail, I'm in charge, and..."

His voice trailed off. He'd meant to say that the South Cliffs were Bailey's strongest supporters, practically her honor guard, but he didn't want to sound boastful and make the other packs jealous.

Roger of the Silver Stars shrugged. "Things change, and we do what we can." He'd recovered from the wounds he'd taken proving his bravery in the temple.

One of the Junipers took a swig of cherry cola. "There've been too many fuckin' funerals," he muttered. "But Fenris willing, there ain't gonna be no more after we're done with this. Not for a while, anyway."

The Juniper Pack was the smallest and most obscure of all those present. They'd also been the first to suffer the Venatori's wrath, with some of their warriors going down against the Order's vanguard and their shaman murdered by a witch shortly thereafter.

Bailey raised a bottle. "Indeed. We're gonna win this, and things will be okay in the long run."

She wondered, though, where Fenris was. He'd mysteriously disappeared during the battle with the first wave of Venatori. She was a full shaman, having been ordained by their god, but she wondered if he was still testing her. Trying to see if she could handle things without him.

Or he might have had important business. If the other gods were angry, she hoped he could soothe their tempers until the conflict was over.

"We're gonna have a witch goddess after us soon," she said aloud. "She's not unbeatable, but things are gonna get tougher before they get easier. Hope you dipshits are ready."

Blustery comments and rumbles of assent wafted off the army as its members ate.

One of the guys from downstate in Oregon—not a Whitcomb, from somewhere even farther south—stood up. "Yeah, well," he growled, "here's what I think of their precious goddess." He unzipped his fly and got rid of some used soda against the trunk of a large tree.

Weres chuckled, sharing the sentiment.

Bailey coughed. "Put that away, you animal. No one would want to see that little thing, even if they could." He was facing away from her, but it seemed like the proper thing to say.

Discussion ensued, but once everyone got bored with dick jokes, it turned to the future.

"So," one guy began, a lean ginger-haired kid from the

Idaho panhandle, "when this is all over, do we get to come back to this place? I probably shouldn't say this, but the Other is fuckin' *awesome*. Like, yeah, this is sacred ground, but it'd be a good place for parties and raves and shit."

Someone threw an empty soda bottle at him, and he cussed up a storm while trying to find the culprit.

"Sit down," Bailey told him.

Alfred, the gray-haired shaman, opined that "We should come here more often. We as a people, I mean. Until this conflict started, we'd been losing touch with our roots, our spiritual heritage. Maybe not come to party, but more wolves should make pilgrimages to this forest. To hunt, and to commune with the woods and the moon and the ancestral spirits who watch over us all."

The mood turned serious, but was by no means unpleasant.

"I'd encourage it," said Bailey.

Having piled the three bodies in the extreme rear corner of Gunney's back lot, Roland disposed of them by conjuring a thick rain of powerful acid. It quickly dissolved them, without sending up telltale plumes of smoke the way fire would have.

The mechanic watched for only a second. "Good God, that's awful." He retched. "Couldn't have happened to nicer people, but still horrible to see. And the smell!"

He turned away, and Roland joined him. "Yeah. But they'll never threaten this town again."

As they regrouped inside the shop, the wizard puzzled out the encounter.

It had seemed too easy. The Inquisitor they'd fought had looked relatively young as well, making him think she'd been a new recruit, maybe an apprentice Inquisitor, and that the one leading the expedition must still be at large.

He doubted the Venatori would have put the mission in the hands of anyone who was less than terrifying. That meant they still had a much more difficult fight ahead of them.

Roland spoke to everyone at once. "What we need to do now is rally the town. Some of them might not even know what's going on, and others are either ensorcelled or terrified. That's where we come in. If we slip around talking to people, we can get the backup we need to take out the other Inquisitor and whoever else she has helping her."

Everyone agreed, although the younger folks—Jon, Trevor, Charlene, and the other two witches, not to mention Dante—were obviously scared. Roland suspected this was their first experience with combat to the death, although they had some skill at fighting.

Gunney sighed. "I guess that means you'll need a vehicle. Hold on a sec."

He grabbed a ring of keys off the wall and drove up a minute later in a Ford Transit van large enough to carry all eight of the crew. As he stepped out of the driver's seat, the mechanic's face was grim.

"This thing," he extrapolated, "is what I use for transporting parts and carrying shit that I don't want to throw in the back of a truck. It's useful to me, so be fuckin' careful with it, okay?"

"Sure." Roland rubbed his chin as he examined their new ride. "You know, this is kinda like the one the A-Team had, isn't it? Wait, or was that a Chevy? Crap."

One of the girls snickered, and Dante rubbed his eyes. "Oh, no. *No*, man. It's not even in the same ballpark. But it's nice to pretend. We can dream, right?"

"*No*," Gunney interrupted. "None of you knuckleheads is allowed to imagine yourselves in an '80s action show right now, doubly so while driving that thing. That's my *van*. If it comes back in pieces, you'll be leaving this shop in pieces. I don't care how much magic you have. I got my ways. You don't wanna find out."

Roland held up his hands, palms outward. "Okay, we get it. Calm down. We just need it for basic transport. We'll bring it back in mint condition. Or near-mint, if we hit a pothole on one of the shitty roads in this town."

Gunney simmered but said no more. Roland motioned for everyone to pile into the van's rear compartment, aside from Dante in the passenger's seat and him as driver.

He sighed while accepting the keys from the mechanic. "I've let Bailey do all the driving lately. I haven't touched my car in, what, a month? The battery might be dead. Anyway, I'm a safer driver than she is, so fear not, old man."

He fired up the engine and pulled out into the road. Then he went uphill into the town's northern fringe, rather than toward the main highway.

They spent the remainder of the day weaving through Greenhearth's side streets and the surrounding network of half-forgotten rural roads. Five times they parked in a hidden nook, piled out, and made conversation with the handful of locals who weren't hiding in their homes. They seemed dazed or oblivious. Roland figured some had been hit with low-level memory wiping spells and used subtle enchantments of his own to jog their minds back toward normality, but otherwise, they simply explained the situation.

Every person they spoke to reacted with varying degrees of terror, usually mixed with anger. They knew what the Venatori's presence meant.

But Roland was also a known quantity and one who was starting to command respect. He'd nearly sacrificed his life to stop the last attack and foil the Order's scheme to turn witchkind against the people of the valley.

And today, with four other Seattle witches by his side, he proved to them that the tide was turning against the European cult. Even their most fearsome operatives could be beaten and *had* to be beaten, because they were well on their way toward finding Bailey's brothers and using them to leverage the shaman.

"Thus," Roland said to the bald guy who owned the hardware store, whom Browne had recently made a sheriff's deputy, "all I need you to do is act as an auxiliary force, maybe provide covering fire. You guys shot a couple of witches before, didn't you? They're as susceptible to bullets as anyone else. We'll do the heavy lifting when it comes to it."

The man rubbed his narrow jaw and squinted into the distance. "Hmm. Okay, fine," he said. "But don't waste time here. You oughta go to Bailey's house and find her brothers."

"The Venatori were already there," Dante pointed out, "so we don't know where they are. But we'll look anyway."

En route to the Nordin residence, they bumped into two more clusters of Weres. One pair was somehow utterly ignorant of the Inquisitor's presence. Roland was about to cuss them out for not paying attention when they explained they'd been on patrol in the woods east of town.

"Hey," Charlene commented, "what about that guy who was suspended in midair?"

"Crap," muttered Roland. "Doug. He wasn't there, was he? The witch holding him must have gone elsewhere. I hope she let him go, but that doesn't seem very probable."

Holmquist put a hand on the wizard's shoulder. "We need to prioritize Bailey's brothers."

The second group of wolves they met, three in all, had run into the witches earlier but had been frozen in place after it was clear they knew nothing. They were afraid to incur the sorceresses' wrath.

"Well," Roland told them, "there's no way *not* to incur their wrath at this point. We need to find Jacob, Russell, and Kurt. Can you guys go look for Doug? He's not hanging in the sky anymore. Be careful."

They weren't looking forward to the task, but recognizing that it was all hands on deck, they bounded off into the trees, circling toward the western road where the suspended prisoner had last been sighted.

The van rambled through the maze of residential streets and old farming tracks. Roland was thankful he'd lived here long enough to have learned the layout of the town's periphery since it enabled him to approach the old farmhouse via a convoluted route the Venatori were unlikely to bother with.

They neither saw nor heard anything untoward when Bailey's neighborhood appeared before them. Roland drove up to the house, then around into the backyard. The Nordins would forgive him for the tracks the van put in the mud, given the circumstances, and it would be wise to hide the vehicle from anyone approaching from the road.

All eight of the Seattleites piled out of the vehicle and inspected the house.

Dante blinked. "The lights are on."

"Obvious," Roland chided, "but true. If the boys are home, they'll hear us approaching. Let's go up to the back door, but be ready for anything."

This could be a trap, he thought. *If Bailey's brothers gave them the slip and are halfway to Portland or Salem by now, I'm sure they'd be just as happy to capture* me *instead.*

He shuddered, recalling an old horror story about what Venatori Inquisitors did to their prisoners, and led the way toward the house.

The back door opened.

"Oh, hi," Jacob called. "Who the hell are all these weirdos?"

All eight of them sighed with relief in unison, probably creating a light breeze.

"Seattleites," Roland quipped. "Don't worry, they're the good guys. Are Kurt and Russell here? And do you even realize what's been going on?"

The Were's strong, stubbly jaw tightened as his face fell in dismay. "Uh-oh. Don't like the sound of that. Come inside, tell us all about it, and have some goddamn coffee. Russell made it."

Roland gave a thumbs-up to his followers. "Russell makes really good coffee. Well, strong, anyway."

"Eeeew," Charlene complained. "Coffee tastes like if you boiled socks and powdered chalk together in the aquafaba from a can of garbanzo beans."

"Yes," said Roland, "that's the point. In any event, I'm sure they also have water. Come on."

The whole group piled into the house.

———

Once everyone was inside, they all (except Charlene) had a cup of coffee and hurriedly conferred about what the hell was going on.

"Bailey's fine," Roland reported as the brothers listened with silent intensity. "Last I heard, anyway. She's in the Other, along with a bunch of pack alphas, lieutenants, and other shamans. She doesn't know what's going on back here. We're trying to buffer her from having to deal with it to give her the breathing room she requires, since she and Fenris and the alphas are working on a plan to lure the Venatori's goddess into a trap. From how they described it, they might succeed. I think we *need* them to. It might be the only way to stop those assholes once and for all."

Jacob lowered his head and massaged his brow with his fingers. Russell stared straight ahead, the muscles of his broad jaw tense. Kurt threw up his hands and let his mouth gape.

"Wow!" exclaimed the youngest of the three. "Lure a

goddess into battle and destroy her. That, uh…yeah. That's *something*, all right. I suppose Bailey is going to be the one to kill her? I mean, it sounds like the kind of thing she would do, but usually someone a little saner would talk her out of it."

Uncomfortable fidgeting went around the group and Roland rubbed his eyes, mimicking Jacob's expression.

"Kurt," the wizard began, "it sounds crazy, yeah, but then again, the whole situation is insane. Fenris knows his shit. I wasn't sure I trusted him at first, but he's always been helpful, and he's almost always right. He believes it can be done, and he believes Bailey is the one who can do it. Last I heard, she's resting and preparing before the actual battle."

Jacob looked up. "We should go there then and help her. She's going to need all the backup she can get." His brothers nodded with obvious enthusiasm.

Roland held up a hand. "Wait. I agree that we should help her, but first, we need to deal with what's going on right in front of us. The whole reason the Venatori are in Greenhearth is that they're planning to use you guys as leverage against her."

The Nordins frowned, but the wizard could see he was starting to convince them.

Charlene raised a hand. "Do you guys have anything to eat? Sorry, but I didn't have lunch."

"Yeah," Jacob said at once. "Let's throw together a quick dinner while we talk about what to do next. We don't have a lot of time, but all the shit we're gonna have to deal with will be harder on an empty stomach."

Mr. Holmquist chuckled. "I agree."

The brothers set to cooking, throwing two trays filled with chicken tenders and potato wedges into the oven while mixing a quick salad for the benefit of anyone who wanted healthier fare (mainly the witches). They set both the kitchen table and the coffee table in the living room for all their guests.

Roland ran back and forth, talking to them as well as Dante, Holmquist, Charlene, and the others about how best to defeat the Venatori. They considered simply waiting for the witches to show up and trapping them at the Nordin house, but that would increase the likelihood of bad things happening to other townsfolk in the meantime.

Kurt had a good idea, though. "You know, maybe one of us—like me, even—should walk around in the middle of town with two or three witches as bait, with everyone else lying in ambush nearby. Then jump 'em."

"Yeah," Dante agreed, "that's how we beat the first group. I think it could work again."

Roland scratched his nose. "Possibly. There's another Inquisitor out there, stronger than the first one, so it would still be risky. But I can't think of anything else that would–"

"Hey!"

Everyone's gaze snapped toward the voice. Charlene was pounding down the steps from the second floor, having gone to the bathroom up there while everyone else took turns using the downstairs toilet. The girl's eyes were wide with fear.

"They're coming up the street toward the driveway!" she exclaimed, her tone thin and strained.

Russell grunted, "How many?"

"Four," the young witch reported. "None of them are wearing black, so I guess only regular ones? Still..."

Roland blinked. "There should only be two or three regulars plus the other Inquisitor. They must have brought in reinforcements since they started scouring the town. Fuck. Uh, everyone hide! Except you guys." He gestured toward the Nordins. "Act like we're not here. We'll spring out at the appropriate moment."

"Goddammit," Jacob grated. "That's not going to work."

The wizard retorted, "We don't have time to come up with anything else, do we? And we have enough people to beat them. Just act, you know, casual."

"Casual." Kurt scoffed. "Sure."

The guests scattered. Roland hid behind the couch in the living room, and Jon and Trevor crowded into the bathroom. Mr. Holmquist stuffed himself into the nearest closet. The other witches ran upstairs.

Someone knocked on the door. Watching and waiting and holding his breath, Roland's eyes fell upon the coffee table in the living room, set with extra plates and utensils.

Oh, shit, he groaned inwardly. *They're going to have to explain that. Please, Jacob and Kurt and Roland,* don't *screw this up.*

Jacob walked to the door and cracked it open.

The witches did not wait for the Were to greet them before they issued their demands. "You," said the one in the lead, pushing the door the rest of the way open and stepping in, "call your brothers. They are here?"

"What the hell?" Jacob protested. "Who are you people? Get out of my house!"

He was, Roland thought, keeping up the ruse well

enough, acting indignant and hostile but not outright fighting back so as not to force the witches' hands toward violence before the trap was ready.

Russell and Kurt rushed up behind him.

"Hey!" the bigger brother rumbled. "What's this shit?"

The four sorceresses in their dark red leather smirked at their prey. "You must come with us," said the apparent leader, a thin, olive-skinned woman with curly dark hair. "It will be easier for you. You know what we can do. If you resist, we will beat you to within an inch of your worthless lives, then strip off your skin while you still live. A skinned wolf will attract the attention we want as well as a whole one."

The other three witches laughed menacingly at that. Kurt started to blurt out a threat, but Jacob held up a hand to silence him.

"Listen," said the eldest, "you can't expect us to go with you without explaining what's going on, but if you want to discuss this, we were just about to have dinner, so we can talk about it over food."

"Hah!" the leader jeered. "You offer us hospitality? And who are those places set for?" She flourished her hand toward the coffee table, and Roland tensed. They might have to spring the attack right away.

Jacob shrugged. "Some of our friends were gonna come over in like, twenty minutes, but it looks like the food is done early. And there should be extra."

One of the witches in the rear murmured something in French, and the quartet all tittered.

"How amusing!" the leader exclaimed. "Yes, let us have dinner. Then we will be leaving. All of us."

They strode across the living area into the dining room. Roland wondered if they suspected anything, or if they truly were as stupid and arrogant as they seemed.

The wizard cast a minor spell to funnel sounds from the table toward himself, and he listened carefully as chairs were pulled out, utensils were rearranged, and the oven door opened, followed by Jacob removing the pans of chicken and fries while Kurt brought out the salad. The sorceresses chattered in their preferred language all the while.

Come on, guys, Roland thought. *Hurry up and give us some kind of signal here. We need you in the fight.*

The brothers set out the food, and the cocky lead witch announced, "Let's tear in!"

"Yeah," Jacob agreed, his voice rising to a far higher volume than necessary, "let's."

Now.

Roland sprang up, using the sound-amplification spell to judge distance as he threw a curving lasso of nonlethal electricity around the bend of the hall and into the dining room. The women screamed and cursed, and a chaotic racket rose all through the house as Weres and witches pounced, flung spells, or rushed in to engage the intruders. The last thing Roland saw before he was immersed in combat was the lead witch gritting her teeth and flinging a plate filled with chicken tenders at Jacob's face.

Bailey was not one to despair or turn down a challenge, but there was no denying basic, factual reality. The battle to come might be the toughest she'd ever encountered.

The woods were swarming with witches, some of whom terrified with the dangerous and domineering aura they gave off.

Bailey strengthened the soundproof arcane dome she'd conjured over her group and fell back thirty or forty feet. She motioned for her alphas to form a huddle. Moving low to the ground with the efficient quickness characteristic of their species, they clustered around her, eyes bright and serious.

"Okay," she began, "the Venatori have finally sent their heaviest hitters. That's why they're in uniform, and also why the witches leading them are wearing black outfits instead of the usual dark red. Plus, I can sense the magical power coming off them. It's the strongest of any I've seen. The regular Venatori are stronger than normal witches, and these new ones are two or three times stronger. Maybe more. At my best, I'm a match for *one* of them at once. All of us together might be able to tackle two tops."

She grimaced as fear spread over the faces staring at her, then added, "But we might be able to separate them and confuse them, stuff like that. I can't think of an ideal strategy yet, though. Does anyone have any ideas?"

The Juniper alpha suggested, "Circle them. Pick off the weaker ones. Get them confused, so they friendly-fire each other? Best I can come up with."

"Eh," Bailey replied, "it could work, but we have to find something that would give us an edge. That's a start, but we need more."

Alfred Warner rubbed his beard. "We can rip a page from one of the oldest books and pretend to be the prey rather than the predator. That worked earlier, albeit against standard witches. Pretend to flee to lure parts of them off, *then* move to circling, hit-and-run, and the like."

Nods of assent followed. The pack's confidence was starting to come back.

Then Will made a further suggestion. "The temple. We could lure them in there and let its defenses do half the work for us."

Bailey felt as though a light went on in her brain, but then a dismal thought came to her at the same time as another wolf, one of Will's buddies, spoke.

"But what about us? Won't we have to deal with all that crap again as well?"

Bailey creased her brow. "I don't think so, believe it or not. We passed the trials. Well, some of you weren't here for that, but you're all with me, and I damn sure passed the temple's requirements. So did Will and Roger and everyone else who was there. We oughta be able to just glide through. The Venatori will send the place into emergency mode, and they'll be pinned down fighting off the ancestral spirits and stuff as we start picking them off."

Will looked excited. "Yeah, definitely. That place is a deathtrap. Everything freaked out when the witches came in after us before. Plus, half of it is a maze, which we navigated, but they don't have a way of getting through it fast. Only one of them made it out alive, and didn't she go into hiding?"

It occurred to Bailey that she had no idea what had become of the young Finnish witch she'd spared. She only hoped the sorceress hadn't gone straight back to her mistresses with useful information.

The Venatori were closing in.

"I'm not sure," the werewitch admitted, "but that's the best thing I've heard so far. All your ideas were good, in fact, so let's combine them. Move out toward the temple, which is that way. We can hash out the details when we're farther ahead of them."

Everyone shifted to cover more ground in less time, and they hurtled through the forest and up the gentle slope toward the plateau near the summit of the massive hill. There, the ancient pyramidal structure housing the primordial spirits of their kind awaited.

Bailey sent out a psychic message to her friends, urging the swiftest wolves to run ahead and then howl when they reached the temple's clearing. Meanwhile, she hung toward the rear of the pack, the better to protect the others with magic if the Venatori got close enough to attack.

The silvery trees sped by on either side of her, the tall grass brushing against her black-furred legs. Stones appeared, carved with hieroglyphs of lupine forms and runes that were indecipherable, yet curiously familiar.

Two howls rose over the forest. Bailey urged the others onward, then shifted back into human form. She stood up and looked straight back—into the eyes of two witches standing a hundred yards away.

"You lose!" the werewitch bellowed. She ducked behind a tree, shielding for good measure, as streams of electrified plasma streaked past. "You've *already* lost, and you'll *never* win. All you ladies might as well go back to Europe before you get yourselves killed."

She threw herself toward the ground, changed shape in midair, and bounded uphill to the sacred site where her pack waited. Behind her, the witches cursed and gave chase, moving at a heavy trot, burning and blasting their way through trees, plants, and rocks as needed.

Up ahead, the werewitch could see the foliage thinning, and she smelled her fellow lycanthropes nearby. Again she reverted to human form, popping her head up just long enough to taunt her foes.

"You failed! I'm still here. You still want me, come and fucking get me!"

She blocked a beam of plasma so powerful it drove her reeling backward and started to burn through the shield almost as soon as it struck. Bailey rolled aside, shifted again, and was running off at an angle when the deadly blast tore through her shield and exploded into the ground.

That was one of the Inquisitors, she surmised. *I used a pretty strong shield. It might be impossible to block their full-power attacks. Shit.*

Bailey burst through the last of the trees and into the clearing at the summit. Her small army of Weres stood there, most of them back in human form, although a few stood on four legs, crouched and ready to pounce. Behind them was the tall stone step-pyramid, and the misty translucent barrier still surrounded it.

She strode toward the wall of fog and spread her hands. It parted without her needing to cast any particular spell, perhaps in recognition of her status as a full shaman. "Come on," she urged her followers. "Get through the entrance before they catch up with us. You saw the size of that explosion."

Werewolves dashed through the opening and into the temple. As the last of them passed her, Bailey saw human figures advancing over the crest of the hill toward the clearing. A woman screamed something in French.

She ducked through the gap and left an arcane shield behind her to be safe. A hurricane of magic crashed against both the mist-wall and her conjured barrier, lighting the clearing up like noon, and the forcefield began to melt away.

Sucking in her breath, Bailey hurled herself through the dark doorway into the temple. The other Weres had begun to descend the great staircase that led down into the subterranean trial chambers, and she urged them to hurry.

The group rounded the corner as the stairs angled to the side and emerged into the broad hall where the Bailey recalled facing the first trial. She was somehow unsurprised when a silver-blue light coalesced in the center of the chamber into a luminous figure shaped vaguely like a wolf.

"Welcome, Bailey Nordin!" it greeted them. "And Alfred Warner. Be at peace during your visit. You may study, meditate, or train as you see fit."

The girl glanced at Alfred and saw that his mouth was hanging open in shock. He quickly bowed his head in reverence.

"Thanks," she said on behalf of them both. "We wanted to bring the whole pack through the maze as a training exercise. Don't need to go through any of the other trials again, though." With a wave of her hand, they all marched across the stone chamber toward the door on the far side.

The specter gazed at her, and she felt a bit guilty. They

were using the temple's guardians to do their dirty work and act as their meat shields, but it wasn't as though the Venatori could kill the immortal spirits of the shamans of the past.

At least, she didn't think so.

Then footsteps thudded above and behind them and the guardian spirit vanished, only to reappear again as a multiplicity of snarling wolf's heads that filled the whole chamber.

"*Intruders!*" it bellowed. "Violators and desecrators, unwanted foes! Remove yourselves from this holy place, or face the wrath of all weredom!"

Bailey hastened toward the black passage at the other end of the hall. "Move," she urged her allies. "Faster."

It had begun.

"Oh?" Roland inquired, raising an eyebrow. "Are you sure about that? Russell, let's make certain she's *sure.*"

The huge werewolf growled as his jaws closed harder on the witch's arm. Screaming and mewling in pain, but mostly in fear, the woman blurted out, "Yes! Yes, it is true. The Inquisitor, Madame Jarvis, and Madame MacLachlan are the only other ones here. The rest of us were all recalled for something. I do not know what. They are waiting on the ridge to the west. If I do not contact them soon, they will begin to destroy the town."

The group all stood around her, watching grimly, four of them bandaging wounds or drinking water to rehydrate after having lost blood. The supercilious leader of the four, named Kasia, and one other knelt on the living room floor. The remaining two lay dead in the dining room. There had been no deaths among Roland's allies.

The wizard glared at her. "How soon? And are the two

of them legitimately powerful enough to wipe out Green-hearth by themselves?"

"Ah," Kasia blinked as she wracked her brain, "perhaps sixty minutes? I have lost track of time since you attacked us. And yes. They are among the strongest witches in the entire Order."

Roland nodded. He was nearly positive the young woman was telling the truth, though he wished she weren't. The news was not encouraging. But it was better to be apprised of the truth than to walk into a difficult fight filled with overconfidence.

"Great." He sighed. "And like I said before, the Inquisitors' reputation suggests that they're nothing to fuck around with. Still, only two of them. This little town has repelled small armies twice before. By rights, we should kill both of you to be safe, but we'll let you live if you behave yourselves. Once your mistresses are dealt with, you can always say you barely escaped with your lives, the usual crap."

The other woman had given no indication of how she felt, but Kasia, like many stuck-up bullies, had proven to be a complete coward once at her foes' mercy, which was convenient. Roland suspected she'd cooperate to save her skin. That just left the silent underling to keep watch on.

Mr. Holmquist, who'd taken a nasty plasma cut to the upper arm, asked, "What do we do now?"

Roland covered the prisoners with a cone of silence before he answered. There was an off chance that one of the captive Venatori might be able to slip a psionic warning to their superiors, so it was better if they heard nothing whatsoever.

The wizard turned toward his allies. "We have approximately fifty-five minutes to raise a small army and take out the two bosses. The good news is that we spoke to enough people on our way here that we should be able to manage it. I can break the enchantments on the ones who were magically dazed. I think. Otherwise, we'll have to make do. We can't allow Bailey to come back to a volcanic crater where her home used to be."

On that much, at least, they were in agreement. But arguments quickly broke out over whether they should risk a direct assault disguised as a diplomatic effort, or try baiting the Inquisitor into following them into the woods, or try intimidating her into leaving.

Roland neutralized the anti-sound cone and questioned Kasia further.

"They are waiting and watching," the witch reported. "On the stony ridge over the road that comes in from due west. They chose that spot because there is no way to approach them except by going straight up the road."

"Figures," Kurt grumbled. "Can't they make it easy, just this once?"

"I know," Dante added. "This is my first time fighting them and I feel like it's been frickin' forever. Still, we gotta do what we gotta do."

After another salvo of discussion, the group agreed to simply assemble as many people who could fight as possible and march most of them straight up the ridge, as a "show of unity" that would conveniently double as an assault force. A handful of Weres would try climbing the cliffs to either side of the ridge to provide minimal flanking when the battle broke out.

Charlene stretched her arms and flexed her hands. "I cannot *believe* we're doing this shit. It hasn't been boring, I'll say that much."

The group marched out of the house and into the town. Dante and Charlene collaborated on a radar-like shield spell that would maintain itself a given distance above and around them while also alerting them to any magical activity with a psionic alarm. They'd have warning if the Inquisitor tried to attack them prematurely.

But no one did. Unmolested, they collected the patrolling Weres they'd spoken to earlier, and a few others besides, their numbers swelling to the strength of a military platoon. Toward the end of their jaunt, they headed toward the sheriff's station.

Sheriff Browne and his deputies came out to meet them with solemn faces, hands clenching their guns. They listened in silence as Roland rapidly summarized the situation.

"We'll come," declared the Sheriff. "Gettin' mighty tired of dealing with these witches every couple weeks. If Bailey thinks she can put a stop to the problem altogether, then it's worth the risk. You all remember to leave us some room to shoot, though. Rifles and pistols don't work the same way as magic and fangs."

Dante couldn't help himself. "Wow, really?"

Browne glared at the boy. "Watch it, son. We don't like smartass out-of-towners here, even if they *are* helping us keep from being turned into charcoal."

The group pressed due west. Another man armed with a carbine and two more volunteer Weres from somewhere to the northeast joined them. They had around forty warm bodies in total, enough for a military platoon, not too shabby against only two adversaries.

Or so they hoped.

As the force approached their destination on the west side, Roland caught a glimpse of Doug, the Were who'd been taken prisoner. He was still hanging helpless in midair, although the witches had moved him back into the woods, which was why Roland hadn't been able to see him earlier.

Well, at least he's not dead yet. Hell, is this going to work? Are we going to accomplish anything except getting half the town killed?

Then he recalled that the entire town was going to get stomped if they did nothing, anyway.

The ridge rose to the right of the western side road, but Roland couldn't discern anyone standing on it. Then, a moment later, two figures appeared on the street, right before it crested over the ridge's far side and vanished into the forested hills. A pair of women, one in black, and one in reddish-brown.

Roland amplified his voice to the level of an announcement, figuring it made more sense to begin the discussion himself.

"Good evening," he began, his voice ringing over the slopes. "We have come, all of us, to negotiate the terms of your departure."

One of the witches' voices came back with a sputtering laugh. "Negotiate! Oh, that's lovely." Judging by the Scottish accent, it was Madame MacLachlan, the telekinesis specialist who'd led the attack on Greenhearth a month-ish ago. "You don't have the high ground, let alone the firepower, so the negotiations won't take long."

The other woman, the Inquisitor, spoke then with an accent Roland couldn't quite place. "We will leave with Bailey's brothers. If you refuse us, you will all die, and this town will be burnt down."

Murmurs of fear and anger went through the massing group. The wizard hoped that the Weres who'd agreed to climb the ridge from the far side were almost in a position to attack, since he was inclined to agree with MacLachlan that the discussion would be brief. Neither of the Venatori seemed in a mood to talk much.

"Well," Roland responded, "what we wanted to say was more like this. We hereby *unanimously* declare that the Venatori Order can fuck right off out of the States, out of the affairs of normal witches as well as all werewolves, and certainly right the fuck out of Bailey's hometown, leaving her family in peace."

MacLachlan started to snort again, but Roland cut her off.

"*And*, by 'her family' I mean more than just her close blood relations. It means all the Weres here and all the people who call the Hearth Valley their home. And me, of course. Oh, and definitely that guy you have floating up there, Doug. Release him too by gently floating him back down to the ground, none of the sarcastic lawyer shit where you let him fall and say that counts as 'releasing' him. Do everything I said, and you'll get back to France in one piece. I'd say that's fair."

The Scotswoman shook her head in disbelief. The

other, Madame Jarvis, only arched an eyebrow, her face coolly disdainful. With a flick of her hand, Doug wafted downwards and slowly came to rest in the grass of the ridge.

"There," she stated. "As for the rest, our terms stand. The brothers come with us. You may have many people with you, but do you think it is enough to overcome me?"

As Roland had expected, their adversaries were refusing to budge. He breathed deep, steeling himself.

"Only one way to find out," he said.

At a snap of his fingers, a swarm of ball lightning appeared a couple of yards behind the two witches, blazing toward them. At the same moment, the Weres all shifted, growled, and launched themselves up the street.

The Inquisitor easily blocked his projectiles despite how close he'd conjured them and them coming from the back, and the other sorceress was raising her hands to attack.

"Shields!" Roland barked.

Dante and Charlene wove a thick, powerful barrier over the group, a mobile one that advanced with the charging wolves and deflected the multi-pronged stream of fire that MacLachlan tossed at them. But she was already using her off-hand to pull an entire section of rock out of the ridge, preparing to roll it down the hill at her attackers.

Roland knew he had to trust his friends' shield and the other witch girl's abilities, to deal with the boulder. Jarvis was about to strike, and whatever she did, it was guaranteed to be devastating.

The wizard harried her with psionic fear pulses and arcane spears from all directions, but the Inquisitor shrugged them off. Then she moved her right arm in an overhead motion as if swinging a sword. Which, in a fashion, was exactly what she did.

A plasma blade the size of a radio tower split the air and descended toward the group. Eyes bulging in shock, Roland threw up the strongest shield he could summon, but it did little more than slow the arc of death slightly and alter its course. Charlene had managed to roll the boulder into a slight ravine, but Jarvis' attack could not be neutralized.

Screams went around the street as Weres, witches, and normal gun-toting townsfolk scattered to the sides or ran backward. The wolves out in front were too close and simply barreled forward, trying to maul the Inquisitor before the blade struck.

Magenta light, flames, and chunks of asphalt flew up amidst the deafening crash and deadly heat. Roland had jumped toward a natural alcove in the cliff to the right, and the shockwave, hot wind, and debris from the impact drove him hard against the rock. He forced himself back out into the open the instant the worst was over, though, since they had no hope in the fight without all of their casters working together.

As he leaped forth, though, something occurred to him. The giant plasma blade had, he realized, in fact been a bunch of smaller blades chained together. The Inquisitor may not have had the raw power he feared, but she was certainly creative at finding ways to maximize the effect of basic spells.

In a frenzy, he began throwing every piece of offensive magic he could think of at the two Venatori, allowing himself only enough rational thought to avoid striking the Weres who circled, lunged, and pawed at the witches. Otherwise his existence became like that of a thunderhead in the middle of a storm.

Nothing had touched the witches at the top of the road. But for all their power, the sheer number of wolves circling them, and the furious onslaught of magical attacks, kept them pressed down. At first, Jarvis and MacLachlan had scarcely broken a sweat, but now both were deep in concentration as they fended off the nonstop harrying.

Still, their power was terrifying.

MacLachlan swept her arms around in wide, flailing circles, tossing lycanthropes through the air to crash against stone, trees, or broken asphalt. She telekinetically picked up chunks of the devastated road, loose stones from the cliff, and entire trees, hurling them like catapult payloads at the endless waves of attackers. Some fled or went down wounded, but they didn't stop.

Jarvis fought in a more controlled way, carefully managing the strikes against her and counterattacking at unexpected moments with blasts that Roland and the other witches found almost impossible to block or redirect.

The street and its surrounding hills had become a war zone, and the chaos of the melee was such that the wizard did not know if anyone had been killed yet. Gunshots sporadically cracked amidst all the other noise as Browne and the other cops fired when it was safe.

The Venatori were forced to engage more frantically. For all their magical skill, they lacked the physical enhancements of Weres and were no stronger than normal humans in close combat. MacLachlan, at one point, accidentally knocked Jarvis off-balance with a clumsy percussive spell, and the Inquisitor destabilized the other witch with a blast of icy wind.

Roland glanced at Doug. Though Jarvis had lowered him to the ground, he was still subtly bound with invisible arcane cords. Yet his eyes were alert, and Roland sensed a vitality in him, as though he'd spent his imprisonment resting and recovering. Everyone had forgotten about him.

And he was positioned in such a way that, if freed, he could pounce on Madame Jarvis' head, given the proper opening.

Before Roland could do anything, MacLachlan seized a huge pine tree, uprooted it, and swung it sideways like a colossal club at a cluster of three Weres. The wizard struck the tree with lightning, shattering it into smoking pieces that still knocked two of the wolves around but probably saved their lives. The third one came down almost on top of the Scotswoman.

"Fuck this!" she cursed, barely swiping the wolf aside. Then a firebolt tossed by Dante streaked past her cheek.

She turned and ran, using magic to amplify her speed, flying when necessary, and disappeared behind a wooded rise. Roland saw a faint glow of deep purple, suggesting she'd opened a portal to escape.

Madame Jarvis gritted her teeth in anger at being abandoned. Even with many of Greenhearth's defenders wounded or tired, she was still a match for all of them. Charlene harried her with random small explosions while wolves tried to snap at her heels or face, and Dante shielded them from her attacks as best he could. Rather than pure destructive power, Jarvis turned to sinking the ground beneath the feet of the lycanthropes, entangling them in vines, or creating pockets of intensely cold air that pained them to enter and impeded their mobility.

"You fools!" the witch barked. "This was your last chance. Even if you kill me, I will take *half* of you with me! And there are far more Inquisitors than I, who will return for revenge!"

Charlene cawed back, "Yeah, big talk for someone who's surrounded!"

Roland sent his mind out toward Doug and sensed the pattern of the spell that kept him bound. With precise surges of counter-enchantment, he unraveled it cord by cord. One of the Were's legs twitched free.

I hope he realizes what I'm doing and what an opportunity he has, the wizard *fretted. If he doesn't, Greenhearth's population is going to end up a lot lower before we have a shot at victory.*

The last arcane cord fell away, and Doug slowly moved all his limbs in place. His eyes were focused on the Inquisitor, the back of whose black-haired head hovered just in front of and below him.

He shifted, surging with adrenaline despite his haggard state, and pounced.

The big furry shape crashed into the witch, who failed to see him coming. Shouts went up as the group realized what had happened. Roland and seven or eight others converged on the sudden struggle. Then Doug was flying back, an ice spear through the center of his torso.

"No!" Roland cried out.

But Jarvis had been too badly hurt and disoriented to recover in time. Other wolves bit into her limbs, pulling her off-balance.

Then the wizard grabbed Dante, Charlene, and the other girl, and the four of them launched a circling blast of concentrated fire and plasma at the Inquisitor's chest. The lycanthropes scattered as it struck, and screaming, Madame Jarvis was incinerated. The noise of battle died down as her ashes fell across the street.

Roland and a cluster of others rushed to the side of Doug.

The werewolf, reverted to human form, looked up at them, chuckling and gasping, with blood on his lips. The giant icicle through his chest was half-melted from his body heat, though he was getting colder. His head tilted back, and his eyes closed.

***

Bailey covered the mouth of the corridor with a chameleon illusion that would make it appear as though there was no exit out of the statue-chamber they'd just left. With the witches inside the temple and the guardian spirits going haywire, the Venatori would have their hands full momentarily. That was when the Weres would launch their first hit-and-run-attack.

Probably not the last. Who knew how long it would take to beat them? She dismissed any notion of "hoping for the best." It had to be done, and it would take as long as it took, period.

The illusion functioned like a one-way mirror. Her position, and that of the wolves behind her, would remain hidden from the witches (at least at first) while she could still watch.

The first of the witches marched into the massive stone chamber. Spirits were taking shape all over the floor and walls and ceiling, moving toward the desecrators.

"You!" echoed the voice of the chief wolf spirit. "Leave now, or be destroyed utterly. We will not allow you in this, our sacred place!"

A woman's voice shouted something back in harsh, metallic-tinged tones of contempt, and the hall flashed with powerful, fast-moving sorcery that Bailey's eye could not follow. The wolf spirit vaporized into a shower of silvery-blue sparks that were reabsorbed into the earth and air of the temple.

But the place's defenders had more to throw at them. Phantom wolves in both bestial and human form hurled themselves at the sorceresses with eons of frenzy behind them.

Bailey held up a hand. "Wait," she whispered. The corridor was too narrow for more than her and one other person, anyway, but she didn't want any of her Weres jumping past her to start the ambush early.

Three witches, all regulars, had advanced beyond the others to try to flank the cluster of angry spirits. A fast, sudden pounce-attack would catch them unaware.

"Now!" Bailey shouted.

She and the three wolves closest to her sprang out of their hiding place. Two converged on one of the witches while she and another wolf leaped toward another, and the third witch panicked and fled back toward her allies.

Bailey and the Were next to her hurled the sorceress in their grasp behind a stone pillar, which offered them limited protection. The witch tried to fire off a flaming blast, but Bailey forced it back into the woman's face, then speared her through the chest with plasma. Off to the side, the other two Weres had ripped the throat out of the witch they'd attacked.

"Back!" the werewitch ordered. She and her fellows scampered into the corridor and moved on to the next chamber as shouts of anger and commands echoed behind them.

It took only a moment or two for the Venatori to clear the chamber and advance into the corridor. The illusion was easily dispelled once they'd seen the Weres emerge from what looked like a bare wall. By then, Bailey and her pack were in the room beyond.

This was the one where, during the trials, they'd had to face the animated statues of the great alphas of the past. Bailey suspected the Venatori would face the same test—except that she and her own alphas would, this time, fight alongside the heroes of old. They hid behind statues, pillars, and braziers, and waited.

Witches streamed out of the corridor. Still the lights and noises made by the temple's spirits wailed and buzzed their warning of doom. Inquisitors directed their subordinates to fan out and cover as much of the chamber as possible before any ambush could be sprung. As soon as they stepped into the great hall, the statues began to crack and their eyes to blaze.

Giant wolves of stone became wolves of spiritually-enhanced flesh. The enraged alpha spirits, given solid form, fell upon the intruders with a bestial fury that chilled even Bailey's blood. She waited for the first shock of their assault to stun the Venatori, then sent out a telepathic signal for her men to attack.

Mortal Weres joined the immortal ones, lashing out and picking off two more of the Order's troops before retreating. Huge and deadly blasts of magic filled the airy space and ricocheted off walls. One unfortunate wolf was caught by an arcing bolt of lightning and fell dead and smoking to the floor. Bailey's heart ached, but there was no time for mourning. She called a retreat, moving into the next corridor as the Venatori struggled to subdue the legendary alphas. They lost at least one more witch before the Inquisitors blasted the guardians into dust.

The pack had moved on. They came to the broad hallway at the beginning of the vast labyrinth that formed most of the rest of the temple.

"Okay," she told her followers, "Will and Roger and I and the others remember this place. Mostly. Follow us. Do *not* get distracted by anything you see or hear. The whole damn maze is full of illusions that'll lead you off into a dead-end or a long-ass detour. There are a couple of were-bears, too. Just run past them. The idea is to get our friends back there to split up, get lost, and lose numbers to attrition. The maze will do half our work for us."

They agreed and waited.

At the first sign of the Venatori leaving the alpha-chamber, Bailey tossed a lightning bolt toward the entrance. A black-clad woman emerged and deflected it with ease, but it had gotten her attention. By the time the other witches joined her, the pack had fled around the corner into the random jumble of halls, intersections, passages, and false walls.

The lycanthropes made good progress. Bailey remembered most of the turns she needed to take, and at the junctures that confounded her memory, the wolves who'd been with her before picked up the slack, guiding them in the correct direction.

Sometimes they paused, waiting for the sounds or auras of their pursuers to grow stronger since they didn't want to get too far ahead. The idea was to string the witches along, remaining slightly beyond their grasp. Shapes and noises occasionally flitted by to the sides, but at Bailey's urging, her allies stuck with her and did not pursue them.

Soon they came to the place where the bear shifter had surprised them during the tests. It was agitated, yet distracted. The temple going into emergency mode had whipped it into a frenzy, yet the Weres were not its target.

"Keep moving!" Bailey called. "Stop beyond that bend up ahead."

They piled around the corner, leaving the giant snarling bear behind them. Bailey peeked out to wait for the Venatori to arrive.

A cluster of witches stomped down the hall. The were-witch noted with satisfaction that the group was smaller than previously. Some of the Venatori had probably split off to chase the scampering illusions, been rerouted to gods-knew-where, or been killed.

In their haste, the Order's agents hadn't considered that they'd encounter other creatures within the labyrinth. The one out in front almost crashed into the hulking bear, screaming as it mauled her. Other witches moved in to encircle and destroy it.

Bailey swiped her hand, signaling her people to attack.

Wolves streamed back around the corner and slashed at the sorceresses with their fangs and claws while the were-witch hurled powerful bolts of elemental magic at the heads of the Inquisitors. Two more regular witches went down.

One Inquisitor blocked and dissipated the offensive spells while a pair of witches turned their fury on the ursine brute, detonating a plasma explosion in the center of his torso that blasted his extremities across the hall and reduced him to little more than a sizzling patch of atomic particles.

With another hand-swipe combined with a mental command, Bailey took her Weres deeper into the maze, fleeing at top speed. They'd picked off still more of their foes, but the Inquisitors had vanquished the werebear with relative ease. It was impossible not to recall the difficulty she and her pack had had in subduing the beast the first time through.

As such, open battle against their nemeses would be suicide until they'd further reduced the witches' numbers and strained their patience to the breaking point.

It occurred to the werewitch that they should eliminate the subgroups that had splintered off to chase the phantoms.

"Hey. Any of you guys remember the way you went when those ghost sounds drew you off last time?"

To her pleased surprise, one of them did, at least roughly. He led them through the twisting halls into a detour along the side of the maze until their delicate hearing picked up footsteps. Bailey motioned for everyone to flatten themselves against the walls just beyond an intersection, and she cast a basic but effective cloaking spell over them all.

Figures stormed around the corner, moving at a trot and muttering in French or other tongues. One Inquisitor was near the lead. Her eyebrows shot up as soon as she'd rounded the corner, sensing that the setup was wrong, and the Weres sprang their trap.

Bailey shifted and pounced on the black-clad leader, conjuring a shield around herself with a plasma spike at the head that punched a burning hole through the Inquisitor's body. The woman had time only for a clumsy burst of flame before she died. Off to the sides, lightning crackled and wind blew through the hall, but the wolves killed their enemies in seconds all the same. Five more went down.

"Move," commanded Bailey. "Back onto the right path. We need to stay ahead of the main force."

They succeeded, although on a couple of occasions, the Venatori grew close enough that Bailey feared they'd have to attempt open battle right there. Somehow, though, they managed to pull ahead again, and reached the end of the maze.

They came to the smaller chamber dividing the first and larger portion of the labyrinth from the latter and smaller. Here stood the two stone daises on which spirits had appeared to confound them with riddles, but no specters materialized. Beyond the platforms were a pair of doorways with obscure signs above them.

"Left," said Bailey. "That was the right way. *Correct* way, I mean."

Will and Alfred went out in front, the other Weres took the middle, and Bailey brought up the rear, the better to shield against any magical attacks that might hurtle toward them. She caught only a brief glimpse of the pursuing witches before she backed around the corner and followed her pack into the second maze.

Although they were tired, the shifters fought like a well-oiled machine, the parts working in conjunction to reach the goals of the whole. They executed more hit-and-run ambushes, picking off three more regular sorceresses, and they now outnumbered the Venatori force by at least two to one, and there were only two Inquisitors left. Bailey could have sworn she'd sensed more in the forest, but it was possible the temple had destroyed some of them.

As the pack neared the end of the maze, the Venatori were strung out with frustration and anxiety, cursing in French or issuing crude challenges and insults in English. They were getting sloppy. They knew they were slowly losing.

Abruptly, the pack took a wrong turn and crashed into the enemy group.

"*Shit!*" Bailey exclaimed, hurling a mass of magic at the witches and feeling the arcane disruption as it crashed into an Inquisitor's attack. She threw small shields in front of her wolves as they lunged at the other witches and sought to divide the force in two.

Pure, desperate effort eclipsed her ability to think rationally about what was going on. Lights flashed, and howls, snarls, and screams echoed through the black stone halls. She saw half the Venatori split off from the others under the onslaught of her pack, while she remained in a tight formation with a handful of alphas and lieutenants who struggled against one Inquisitor and two regular witches.

The regulars died under the shifters' assault as Bailey tried to overcome the leader with a storm of six or seven different types of magic. The Inquisitor had trouble counterattacking, but nothing Bailey threw at her got past her defenses.

Then her alphas, including Will, all pounced on the black-clad witch at once. She was battered against the wall and took several nasty claw wounds, but she retaliated with a static-sonic pulse that flung the Weres back, stunned and hurt but not dead.

Bailey lunged at the Inquisitor. In the split second before they clashed, an idea popped into her head.

I'm not just a shifter who can turn into a witch or a Were. I can be both at once. A werewolf is stronger than any normal human or any caster.

Instead of fighting fire with fire, she used magic to augment her skill in melee combat. Her limbs lashed out with a speed and force unknown to most living things. She wrapped arcane shields tightly around her arms and legs and face, each punch or kick or headbutt coming in like a missile.

The Inquisitor retaliated with an awful wave of electricity, radiation, supersonic noise, and psionic despair, but Bailey powered through it despite the agony and nausea that shot through her.

By now, her wolves had rejoined the fray. One of them seized the Inquisitor's ankle, and the brief distraction was enough. Bailey threw the woman into the wall with so much force she wondered if the stone might crack. The witch avoided death from the impact, but she collapsed to the ground, dazed and half-conscious. Will descended on her and ripped her throat out with his teeth.

Bailey motioned for them to follow her. "Come on. We need to move. How many are left?"

The other wolves, the ones who'd split the Venatori's party, came back into sight, running at top speed. One shifted back into human form. "One," he breathed. "The last one in black."

The Inquisitor appeared around the corner. Bailey raised a barrier at the same instant the witch filled the corridor with blazing death.

The werewitch kept channeling magic into her shield, regenerating it as the Inquisitor's massive attacks burned it away. Her wolves scampered ahead of her into the temple's final chamber. The girl forced the shield ahead, turning the witch's magic back on her, then ran into the room with her friends.

It was the square all-white one where she and her pack had confronted their doppelgangers. The place shone with an intense light that was weirdly sinister, but no mirror-image phantoms manifested before them.

The final Inquisitor burst through the door in a cloud of flame and lightning.

"You are trapped like rats!" she bellowed. Her eyes were bloodshot. "Surrender! I will spare the rest of you if you turn Bailey over for–"

Alfred Warner tossed a stream of electrified water at her face. "No deal," he stated.

The witch blocked it with ease, but the wolves nipped at her heels as Bailey struck at her with lightning and ice from above and below and manipulated the very structure of the floor to throw the sorceress off-balance. Then she hurled herself at their last foe.

Again she wondered if she was crazy. The Inquisitor threw out a ring of concussive force to drive the wolves away, focusing her wrath on the werewitch. Bailey met her flurry of plasma blades in kind, and also kicked and lunged at the woman, using her shifter strength to her advantage. Magic crackled against magic, but it was a simple trip-kick to the woman's ankle that finished her.

She collapsed to the floor and wolves swarmed over her in an instant, tearing at her limbs and crushing her skull between powerful jaws. The only sounds were of snarling beasts.

Gasping and trying not to faint, the werewitch slumped against the wall. Her remaining wolves panted and looked around. They could scarcely believe it was over.

The alarm noises made by the temple faded away. They'd been going on for so long that the Weres hadn't noticed them until they were gone. Bluish-silver light took shape near the center of the white chamber.

"Bailey Nordin," said the wolf spirit, "thank you for your help in defeating the desecrators. You have in a sense passed the trials all over again, a rare achievement. We shall now send you and your pack back to the clearing, including those who have fallen. Go in peace and health."

The spirit grew in brightness, and the lycanthropes covered their eyes as the white light engulfed them. After a faint dizzying tingle, they found themselves standing on the plateau again between the pyramid's entrance and the forcefield of enchanted mist. The Weres who'd died in the fight were arranged around them in a circle.

"We made it," a voice behind Bailey gasped.

"Not all of us," she clarified, "but they died as heroes. We wiped out some of the Venatori's strongest forces today. I think we need to honor them, and then we need to head back to our camping grounds and get a little rest. Finally."

CHAPTER TWELVE

M r. Holmquist, despite being from Seattle, delivered the final eulogy.

"Our friend Doug," he concluded. "I never met him before today, but he died to save all of us, helping Weres avoid the same thing that happened to my son. We'll remember him. We'll remember everyone."

The crowd nodded. It was dark, but the Weres, using their strength and excellent night vision, filled in the grave and left Doug in peace beneath the boughs of the pines.

Against all odds, the two witches they'd taken prisoner at the Nordin house had remained crouching at the edge of town, where they'd watched the battle. Roland kept his word and released them.

"Don't come back, please," he suggested. They nodded and hurried into the forest to teleport themselves some-place far away.

The somber mood lifted in part as the massive group dispersed, with most going their separate ways back to their homes or businesses. The sheriff and his men remained on the west road to put up orange signs and cones, though few people drove that way anyhow since it lay off the highway.

Roland, the Nordins, and the various Seattleites remained together. They drifted toward the Bristling Elk.

Jacob sighed as the diner came into view. "I can't believe those fucking witches ruined our food. We gave them our dinner, and that bitch threw it in my face!"

Dante shook his head. "I know, right? Isn't there some stereotype of the French being assholes?"

"Hey!" Kurt protested. "Don't be bigoted, you miserable redneck."

"Sorry," said Dante.

Charlene chimed in. "Yeah, Seattle is definitely a back-woods kinda place with lifted trucks and gun racks every-where. Trust me."

As they stepped into the Elk, Roland kept silent, reflecting on the question of where his home was now. He'd lived his whole life in Seattle, but these days, Green-hearth was the place he cared about most. Still, he was glad to see residents of both towns coming together.

Tomi saw them and asked, "What the hell was going on out there? Did we get attacked *again?*"

"Kinda," Roland replied. He summarized the situation, and the waitress blinked in surprise as she led them to a cluster of tables. The diner was closing soon, but Roland figured that they'd earned the right to a late meal after saving the place and the rest of the town from total destruction.

As they waited for food and then tore in, the conversation turned into a verbal rugby match between species. No one wanted to talk about what they'd just been through or what lay ahead.

"So," Charlene remarked, "clearly you guys can fight and know a thing or two, and you know how to cook. I guess I'm surprised since, I mean, back home, we always kinda thought that Weres were one step up from magical furries and the source of lots of that god-awful Rule 34 shit on the Internet."

Half the crowd, including most of the Weres, burst out laughing at that.

"Bullshit," Jacob countered. "Though I guess it's only fair since we pretty much figured that witches were all one step up from California girls named Karen who had crystal and sage collections and were incapable of doing anything useful."

More laughter. Roland noted an edge to it, but it was for the best that the two groups vented their age-old hostility at a time when they'd befriended each other and were only joking.

They lingered in the diner 'til closing time, leaving Tomi an extra-large tip for the inconvenience, then spilled out into the street.

Roland sighed. "I think we should hang around for a while. Patrol the streets, not acting too vigilant, as a way of reassuring the locals that everything is okay."

It occurred to him that Fenris ought to be here. Where was he, anyway?

Jacob nodded. "Not a bad idea. That includes you, though. People trust you after all that's happened, and the more friends we've got around at a time like this, the better."

Bailey stretched her legs out on the grass and basked in the cool, refreshing breeze that blew through the silvery woods. It felt like it had been only an hour since they'd left the temple, but an obscure property of the holy ground beneath her made her feel like she'd slept all night.

The Weres around her joked and laughed in low voices or discussed what they'd seen and done inside the pyramid. Dog-tiredness lingered in a handful of them, and others seemed shell-shocked, but they were all coping well enough in their own ways.

After a time, the alphas started to look at Bailey.

She rubbed her eyes and inhaled. "I suppose you want me to say something, and I will. You all did well and fought bravely. I'm proud of you. Sorry as I am to have lost anyone, there's no way that won't happen, and it's for a damn good cause. I think we've bought ourselves time, but it's not over yet."

Alfred asked, "Are you still planning to kill their goddess? If it can be done, I have little doubt it will cripple the Order. But realistically, it took us to the limits of our abilities today, defeating that goddess' mortal servants."

A hush fell over the group. Bailey didn't allow it to linger.

"Yes," she stated. "That's still the plan, and it's the best plan we've come up with. Fenris believes it'll work, and he's never been wrong about anything this serious. He's gone over the process with me, and we know how we're gonna go about it, but there's no way of being sure what'll happen. Trust me, we can win. But at the end of our preparations, we're still facing down a pissed-off deity. If some of you don't want to be around for that, I won't blame you."

The pack was quiet for the span of a heartbeat or two.

Will spoke first. "We'll be around. We'll see this thing through to the end."

A quarter of the Weres looked nervous, but none disagreed with the South Cliff alpha's proclamation. They all had committed to remaining by their shaman's side.

Bailey closed her eyes. "Thank you. Not to be too humble, but I honestly couldn't have done it without you. My powers only get me so far when I'm alone." She looked at them. "I was hoping Fenris would show up, but maybe Roland needed his help. Let's go home. We should see our families and get some rest before the next phase."

She stood up, concentrated on the front driveway of her own house, and pulled a shimmering amethyst gateway open in the air before her.

Alfred cocked an eyebrow. "You can open portals this early in your education? Impressive."

"Yeah," Bailey acknowledged. "Mostly, my magic is combat or defense-oriented so far, but I figured that out a while ago. Let's go."

To demonstrate her confidence that the gate led where it was supposed to, she was the first one to step through.

———

Will waved goodbye, nodding to the weres—and witches— who'd defended his hometown while he was gone. "We'll be back," he promised.

"I know," said Bailey.

The alphas and lieutenants separated, departing the Nordin house to visit their families or friends, get something to eat, or catch what precious hours of sleep they could. Once they dispersed, Bailey turned back to her brothers, her boyfriend, and the squad he'd recruited in Seattle.

"Again," she told them, "thanks so much for what you did here. We won't forget this."

Mr. Holmquist nodded. "It's worth it."

A surge of anger came out of nowhere as the girl contemplated the magnitude of all that had transpired. "I should've been here. We *knew* they'd come after our homes and families, goddammit. I don't know. Maybe I could have used those astral clone things to lead the other Venatori into the temple anyway, while the real me was back here where I belong."

Jacob came up beside her, and before she knew it, they were hugging.

"Hey," he said, "don't worry. We handled it. We lost poor Doug, but it's a damn miracle he was the only one. And we took out one of their strongest witches. We're winning, and the town still stands, right?"

She sighed. "That's true."

After a moment had passed, Dante stepped up, flipping his platinum hair away from his face. "So, I was able to scrounge up these miscreants as a resistance party," he explained, "and they were enough—thanks, guys!—but, like, I could have gotten even more people with more time. What I mean by that is, there are a lot more who feel the same way throughout the Pacific Northwest. We could raise a legit small army if we need to."

"Hey," Kurt quipped, "we already have a small army of Weres. With a small army of witches added to it, it'd be more like a *large* army."

Jacob shoved his younger brother. "Good job, Kurt. We definitely needed that clarified. Anyway, I'm gonna guess my sister will approve of that plan, Dante."

"I do," she said. "And shortly, we'll decide when and where and how. But first, have any of you guys seen Fenris? He disappeared right when things got real."

Roland shook his head. "I was wondering the same thing. He helped us get to Greenhearth after I summoned him, but he went off somewhere after that. Must be doing god stuff."

The girl put her hands on her hips. "Well, we need him, so time to summon him again." She looked up at the sky. "*Fenris!* Can you hear me? Come back. We need your help."

Roland cleared his throat. "Summoning a god is usually a *bit* more complicated than that."

A tall figure stepped around the side of the house.

"Bailey," a deep voice intoned. "Forgive me for leaving, but there were things I had to look into, and you know I could not have directly aided you anyway."

She had to admit she was happy to see him. "Glad you're back all the same. Listen, we beat back the Venatori once again, but now we have to decide what to do next. Dante here has a plan you should hear."

The young wizard repeated what he'd told Bailey.

"I see," Fenris mused. "A small army of sympathetic witches? If you're confident about that, I approve."

Dante beamed. "I am, especially after what we've been through." He glanced at the others, mainly Charlene.

The wolf-god gave a faint smile. "Dark times indeed have come when we're forced to consort with casters. Sorry, that was a joke."

Kurt's jaw dropped. "Fenris made a *joke?* Holy crap. Someone check and see if they need a space heater in hell."

Russell prodded his brother in the ass with his foot. "Ow," Kurt complained.

"Well," Dante responded, "we felt much the same way until recently. Let's say that things have changed."

"They have," Fenris acceded. "Soon, I will aid you in opening the portals you'll need to recruit this army. But first, there are things we need to discuss. In fact, the more allies we have for the final struggle, the better."

Bailey frowned. "Not sure I like the sound of that."

The hooded man leaned closer, and his voice was just above a whisper. "A thing long rumored has proven to be true. I was investigating it before I returned to you. The Inquisitors, for all their power, are not the most dangerous of the Venatori's servants."

Roland sputtered, "*What?* You have *got* to be fucking kidding me."

"I'm not," said Fenris. "Though few in number—six, perhaps seven total—they also possess witches or wizards called Dreadknights, whose existence has been kept secret even from most of the Order. Only the former Grand-mistress, her second-in-command, and the Dreadknights' handlers know about them. Along with their goddess, of course."

Charlene snapped her fingers. "I heard of them like, *once,* but I assumed it was BS. Aren't most of them supposed to be from ancient or medieval times?"

"Yes," said the were-deity. "Two of them are among the living, although they may be older than most mortals. The others have been kept in a state of suspended undeath throughout many centuries. I suspect that one was created by Aradia when she first founded the Order. They are adept at *every* known form of magic, as well as having permanent bodily enhancements that make them at least as strong as Weres and exceedingly difficult to kill."

An awkward silence set in, and Bailey was pretty sure she heard the first few crickets of summer chirping somewhere out back.

"Great," she muttered.

"Don't despair," Fenris added. "We have a hard fight ahead of us, but it can be done. Still, we must be prepared for the inevitability of the Dreadknights accompanying Aradia when we challenge her to a direct confrontation. If such is the case, then having overwhelming numbers might be the only thing that tips the scales in our favor."

The girl sighed. "Then that's what we'll do."

Fenris smiled but held up a hand. "Not tonight. I've observed their movements, and the Venatori are regrouping. Again, we've dealt them a major defeat, and they don't have the means to press another attack for at least two days. You have all been through much. I suggest you rest and relax. We'll recruit more troops tomorrow or the day after."

Mr. Holmquist, in a tired voice, seconded the motion. "Great idea. I've kept up with you kids so far, but a man my age needs his sleep. And I suppose I should call the wife and tell her I'm okay but spending the night."

The wolf-god turned away. "I will perform preliminary

scouting so that when we reunite, I can update you on the situation. Call me if you must. Farewell."

He walked into the shadows and was gone.

Jacob breathed deeply, then whistled. "Well, I dunno about the rest of you, but I think we could all use a drink. The Elk's closed, I think, but I believe in being prepared for emergencies."

He led the crowd into the Nordin house, where he busted out a pair of bottles of high-grade whiskey and assembled a line of glasses.

"All we got to chase it with," he pointed out, "is Coke, which in my humble opinion interferes with the flavor, but it's there if you want it."

He poured drinks for everyone save Charlene, who insisted she was a teetotaler. "I appreciate the offer, though." The young witch shrugged.

Jacob took the glass he'd meant for her and looked instead at his youngest brother. "Kurt, I think tonight's the night you become a man. Well, partially, since we all know you're still a virgin."

"Hey!" Kurt protested.

"But," the eldest brother went on, "this is a start. Just don't tell Sheriff Browne, okay? Officially your first drink is another, uh, fifteen months away."

Kurt accepted the glass. "Pffft. Would I do such a thing?"

They all downed their whiskey, some passing around a two-liter bottle of cola as well.

"Oh," Jacob commented, "and Bailey, no fighting."

She scowled at him. "Yeah, yeah, whatever."

Bailey waved and called, "Hi, Gunney!"

"Bailey," he replied, whipping his cap off before returning it to his head. "Come on over. As usual, glad to see you're still alive, even though you seem to be good at not dying. I'm not sure how the hell the rest of us made it through yesterday."

She strolled through the bay door and entered the shop. "Hi, Kevin. Hi, Gary," she greeted the junior mechanics.

Gary gave her a nod and a wave with his wrench. Kevin's voice returned the hail from the ebon recesses of the pit.

Bailey pulled Gunney away from his work to give him a big hug. "You knew you weren't gonna get out of this," she informed him.

He sighed. "I guess not. So, tell me, is it over? Did we win? I've had about enough craziness these past couple months to last the rest of my years, however few those might be."

The girl snorted. "You'll still be here, plinking away at a goddamn Edsel when you're ninety-five. But sorry to say, no. It's not over yet. We're gonna put an end to it soon. I promise."

The older man gestured toward the office. "We started early, so I'm about ready for a lunch break even if it's only ten in the a.m. I got two hoagies in the fridge, steak and cheese, if you want one. And I'm pretty sure my guests yesterday left your orange sodas alone, and we got some good root beer, too."

"Sounds good," Bailey replied, although she'd had

breakfast only two hours ago. "And I think I will have the root beer this time. It's been a while."

Kevin's voice wafted up. "Aww, I wanted root beer."

"Well," Bailey shouted back, "how long's it been since you had an orange soda? I'll donate mine in this case."

"Fine," the voice grumbled.

As the young woman and the mechanic ate and drank, they filled each other in on the details each had missed.

"Jesus H. Christ," Gunney almost moaned. "I knew some bad shit was going down on the ridge last evening, but nothing like that. And you're luring a goddess into a trap?" His face tightened and turned red with anger. "Damn those bitches and their bitch of a goddess. Pardon my French, but we've all had it up to here with them. Fucking dominatrixes and Inquisitors and pagan deities and what, *undead knights*, you say? The hell with all that. Sounds cool until you have to deal with it."

The girl chuckled, suddenly feeling weary, as though she were his age. "Ain't that the truth."

The man shook his head and took another bite. "I miss the old days when all you did was show up and help me work on cars, and that was that. Things were nice and boring and peaceful."

Bailey took a swig of root beer. "I kinda do too. I mean, I'm glad I'm a shaman now, but I'd like things to go back to normal too. Mostly. In fact, even though I have stuff to do, let's work on that Model T or whatever else you got going after we're done. Just for a bit."

"Sure," said Gunney. They finished their simple meal and wandered back into the repair area. The mechanic gestured to the Model T. "As you can see, I painted it while you were away. Nice cheerful red, or at least, that's how it looks to me."

"I like it," she commented.

"All that's left at this point is the interior console installation and wiring. Shouldn't take too long. Lend a hand, grease monkey." He tossed her a rag.

She caught it. "I'll pretend you didn't say that."

They worked mostly in silence, talking here and there of the weather and how they both suspected it would be a hot, sticky summer. Their seasons tended to mildness, but no one could ever be sure.

Soon the remaining tasks were done. "Okay," said Gunney, "start it, and that's that." He handed the keys to his employee.

Bailey arched her eyebrows. "You're not, uh, giving me this car too, are you? Hell, I've barely been able to drive the Camaro yet. Been doing too much of my travel via magic portals lately."

The old man chuckled. "Let's say I might be willing to lend it to you. Then perhaps we'll see if one of your brothers or your boyfriend could use a new ride. I dunno, I'm feeling generous. Kick this witch-goddess' ass, save this town, and when all is said and done, well, we can talk it over."

CHAPTER THIRTEEN

There had been no word from Fenris all day, and Dante had spent much of his time hitting up the Internet from the town library's computer to do his preliminary recruiting. The other Seattleites had passed the hours mingling with the locals, including Weres, and learning the ins and outs of the town's culture. Not to mention its geographic defensibility, in case they were invaded again.

Bailey had spent time talking to all of them, staying abreast of the situation and bolstering morale. As the afternoon faded, she found there was nothing that needed immediate doing.

She and Roland had a brief picnic behind the pole barn and stared at the wooded hills while they ate. The damage done to the forest during the fights with the Venatori was still visible. It might take years to heal.

"You know," she told the wizard, "I don't regret the way things have turned out, but let's say that I hope we can get the good stuff back. This town being a dull, quiet little haven."

Roland rubbed her shoulders. "I think we will. Once the Order no longer can or wants to pursue this insane vendetta against you, there's no reason for anyone to pay much attention to Greenhearth. Which is a good thing."

With her brothers out helping clear the debris from the shattered western road, she soon found herself lying on her bed in her room, with Roland sitting near her feet.

"Hey." She prodded him with her bare toes. "What do you think it will mean for us when this is all over?"

He leaned back, bringing himself closer to her. "Oh, we'll have more time to spend together for one thing, but that's obvious. We might occasionally get bored, but you said earlier that you *want* things to be boring around here. That would be for the best. We can always visit Portland and Seattle if we need to."

"Dumbass," she teased, poking him with her fingers. "You know that's not what I meant."

"I do?" He seemed genuinely confused. She recalled that he was a man and that, according to most other girls, men tended to suck at understanding...anything, really.

Grumbling with exasperation, she spelled it out. "How many couples do you know who come from the same backgrounds as the two of us?"

"Oh." He nodded. "Let's see… None."

"Right," she confirmed. "I'm thinking, well, how are people gonna react? Everyone already thinks I am weird since I didn't want to get married to one of my own kind at the usual time like I was supposed to. I wonder if the situation we're dealing with will make people a little more amenable to the possibility of us, uh, being together for a while."

He folded his hands behind his head and lay on his back next to her. "We've already gotten Weres and witches helping each other out. I don't think anyone will care. And if they do, we get a pass anyway because we're special."

She laughed. "That's technically true, isn't it? We're each the local oddball. Plus I guess we're heroes. Makes it easier than if everyone hated us. Would you still..." she swallowed, "still want to be with me if everyone *did* hate us?"

He rolled over on his side, facing her. "Yes." He planted a kiss on her mouth. "I'm glad they *don't*, but if that were the case, we'd run away to Tennessee or Singapore or who knows where and change our names or something."

Bailey smiled. "I'd rather be around my family. And friends. But I'm glad you have that level of—" She stopped herself. "I was about to say 'commitment,' but I hear guys don't like that word."

Roland shrugged. "It's possible that I'm warming up to it." He pulled her close to him, and their lips met again, and their hands wandered.

Bailey and Roland were up by 6:52. They'd just poured themselves cups of Jacob's coffee when someone knocked on the door.

"Uh-oh," Kurt snarked.

Jacob answered it. "Hi, uh, Agent."

Velasquez gave a sharp nod. "Hello. May I come in? I need to talk to Bailey."

The eldest Nordin boy opened the door wider and stepped aside. "It'd be illegal for me to say no, wouldn't it?"

"Correct," said the agent. He strode over to the couch, and the werewitch and the wizard looked up at him with bleary eyes. "I have information for you."

"Good morning," Bailey drawled. "Jacob, get the man a mug of coffee since he obviously got out of frickin' bed five minutes ago."

Velasquez almost smiled. "Not quite. Listen. I was able to personally contact Aradia under the pretense of inviting her to eliminate you."

Roland spat out his coffee. "You did *what?*"

Bailey put a hand on his arm. "Hold on. Getting her to attack me was always part of the plan, after all." She looked at the agent. "Okay, then. Details?"

After accepting a steaming mug from Jacob, who along with Russell and Kurt watched him with wary eyes, Velasquez related how he'd gotten patched through to the goddess and convinced her that the Agency wanted the "shifter threat" taken care of, with them supposedly turning a blind eye to the whole affair.

"Obviously," he added, "it was a lie. We do plan to aid *you* in destroying *her*, rather than the reverse."

Roland raised his mug as if making a toast. "*That's* good to know."

Velasquez continued, "We are aware that the Venatori dispatched their Inquisitors and you had some difficulties with them, and we apologize for any inconvenience. We're glad you're safe. However, all this was probably inevitable. The idea is to bolster Aradia's confidence so she oversteps herself and comes after you in the Other, where we can assure zero collateral damage, and then be rid of her. At which point, the tensions between the greater communities of both witches and Weres will have time to simmer down. The alliance you've forged is a good sign."

"Thanks," Bailey replied. "And while I'd rather have heard about your plan beforehand, I'll agree it was a good one."

"Yes." The agent sipped his coffee. "Your brother makes this stuff well. My compliments."

Russell grunted in irritation as Jacob shouted, "Thanks!" from somewhere toward the kitchen.

Velasquez elaborated further. "Neutralizing the witch-goddess will provide the best outcome for everyone except the Venatori, and frankly, fuck them. Our organization will benefit nearly as much as you people will. Things will go back to normal, and agent mortality will decrease by a significant margin. For now, I've convinced my superiors to shutter other, lesser operations in the western sector and shift personnel over to aiding you during the coming battle. We should have a large number of combat-ready units available. Fighting a goddess is nothing to trifle with, and it's in our best interest to ensure your success since if Aradia survives, she'll want revenge on us all. That could make life extremely difficult."

"No shit," Roland agreed.

"Agent," said Bailey, "thank you. I've got your number. Stay in touch. Today we'll be recruiting more witches from around the region to help us, and then we'll issue the challenge. If Aradia doesn't find us first."

Velasquez shook their hands and went to his car,

driving off at an unsafe speed on whatever his next errand was.

Jacob watched the man go, then turned to the couple. "You guys should have breakfast before you leave. I made an entire dozen eggs."

"Sure." Bailey squinted. "We still need Fenris back too. Roland, get me some eggs. I'll be right back."

She marched outside, cupped her hands over her mouth, and shouted, *"Fenris!"* into the sky as loud as she dared. Then she sent her mind out across the Northwest and into the Other, willing the deity to hear her call.

Nothing happened. She resolved to eat something, then attempt a proper magical procedure, but when she went back inside, Kurt was opening the back door. Heavy footsteps moved into the house.

"Here I am," said Fenris. "I believe I've learned all I can for the time being. Are you ready for battle?"

Bailey sat down at the dining room table and scooped eggs onto a piece of toast with her fork. "Not quite. We still have to talk to the witches Dante mentioned. He did the preliminary stuff online yesterday. Think you can handle portal duty?"

"Of course," the hooded man answered her. "We should move quickly, though. The Venatori are pulling all their available forces on the continent toward Oregon. And I suspect Aradia may have intuited my actions since she's created a cloud of interference masking her movements. That means she might be preparing to manifest in your backyard. Not that I mean to alarm you, but that's the reality of the situation."

Roland grunted. "To save time, Bailey and I will shower together. Then we'll snap to it."

Jacob shot him a squinty look. "That's my sister you're talking about."

The wizard blinked in mock innocence. "I thought I was talking about efficiency and water conservation."

Twenty-five minutes later, Bailey, Roland, and Fenris stood in front of the house.

"For starters," the werewitch said, "portal us to the middle of town. It'll save a few minutes. Then we can gather Dante and everyone else, and from there, head off to Seattle."

"Done," said Fenris.

Dante gestured. "Okay. This is the place."

Bailey peered at it. "A frozen yogurt shop. Man, I knew even less about the ways of witchcraft than I thought."

"What," Roland marveled. "You telling me you don't like frozen yogurt?"

"More partial to ice cream," she admitted.

Dante waved a hand. "They've got gelato, too. Anyway, come on. The two chicks I was talking to earlier said they'd be here most of the afternoon, plus there's always someone hanging around, so we might get a third, a fourth, or more."

At present, their group consisted of Bailey, Roland, Dante, Charlene, three other witches, and one other wizard whom they'd recruited elsewhere in Seattle. The others were off on similar missions.

Dante had led them through a variety of places on his recruitment drive. Two clubs, one of which Roland had never heard of. A suburban mall where witches often hung around the antique stores. A New Age supplies outlet. A small library, not unlike the one where Bailey recalled going with Roland to test her magical potential. And finally, a line of business suites adjacent to the university.

They pushed through the door. A bell rang, and Dante waved to the guy behind the counter. "Hi. We'll buy something in a minute, but first, we're here to meet people."

"Okay." The employee shrugged.

In the rear corner sat two women, one about Roland's age, the other in her mid-thirties or so. They were attractive in a slightly esoteric way and dressed in normal clothes.

Dante introduced himself, then the others. "And this is Bailey and Roland. I get the impression they're kinda famous by this point."

"Indeed," said Deanna, the older of the two. "We weren't sure what to make of you two at first, but we've all heard about what's been going on lately."

The other witch, named Shari, nodded. "Yeah. It's scary as shit. Nobody's safe anymore, and the Order is causing problems for everyone."

They ordered frozen yogurt and talked as they ate it. Bailey wished the two sorceresses would show more haste, but she understood they needed to feel like they could trust the newcomers before they committed to anything.

Fortunately, it didn't take long. The werewitch suspected that Deanna and Shari had simply wanted to make sure they weren't being scammed or led into a trap.

The other casters vouched for Bailey's reliability and integrity.

"We'll help you, then," the older one concluded. "The last thing witches need is for the general public to start hating us again, just because of what the Venatori are getting up to."

Bailey extended a hand. "Great. Shake on it?"

That seemed to amuse them. For a second, the were-witch felt like the backwoods hick she was, but she shook off the thought. There were far more important things to worry about.

Next, they collected another pair of Weres, a couple Roland had spoken to previously. Both were strong and around forty, and they seemed starstruck once they saw Bailey.

"Goddamn," said Bill, the first. "Me and my wife heard about you, girl. You might be the biggest thing to happen to weredom since...shit, I can't remember."

The woman, Laurene, smiled and clasped the were-witch's hand. "It's an honor to meet you, seriously. You've done so much good."

Bailey thanked and welcomed them. It occurred to her that urban Weres, having assimilated into human society, had a less pronounced division of the sexes than the traditional rural packs did. Among country wolves, it was rare for the females to participate in any kind of fighting except as a last resort. Not counting her, of course.

Having finished in Seattle, they called upon Fenris to open a portal back into the Other, and from there, they moved on to Tacoma, Olympia, Portland, Salem, and Eugene. Only one stop in each, since none had a witch community the size of Seattle's, and most of the Weres in the Pacific Northwest had already joined them.

With daylight waning as they completed their tasks, they opened a portal to Greenhearth with a respectable force of forty-nine able bodies. Bailey imagined she could combine them with her allies from the Hearth Valley and manage the equivalent of a military company.

She only hoped it would be enough.

"Fenris," Bailey asked before they stepped through the gate, "are we going to do it tonight?"

He looked at her with a blank, steady expression. "If you're ready, I think it would be wise. Aradia will strike soon if we don't move first."

The girl closed her eyes, breathed in through her nose, and exhaled through her mouth as she walked through the shimmering door and emerged in a small park of Main Street back home. The others filed out behind her.

A crowd of locals had formed off to the sides since right in the middle of town was a cluster of men in black fatigues and helmets carrying bright silvery-chrome weapons. Their presence was obviously making the towns-folk nervous. They kept staring at them and whispering to each other.

Bailey, though, was happy to see that Velasquez had come through. She walked forward, seeking him.

The lean bronzed man noticed the girl and turned away from his troops to greet her. "Hello, Bailey. As you can see, we're ready."

"Wow," she quipped. "For once, you guys are in town *before* us. We kinda assumed you'd make another dramatic last-minute entrance in the middle of the battle."

Velasquez's mouth took a sour twist. "Ha-ha. The higher-ups have finally realized how serious this is. The force I have at present is smaller than the ones we deployed before, but these are our most elite guys. Two dozen of the best. It looks like you rounded up a good forty or so. Can you depend on anyone else here joining us?"

"Yes," she replied. "Give me an hour."

He nodded. "Are we planning on letting the games begin tonight?"

She flexed her hands, banishing the tiredness she felt through an act of will. "Yessir. Unless anything weird happens. I'd much rather we choose the arena ourselves and have time to get into position and all that. If Aradia attacks first, it'll probably be while we're in bed or sitting on the john or something."

"Agreed." The agent grunted. "Call me in one hour, then."

"Deal."

Since Bailey had previously informed most of the valley about what was going on, nobody needed much time to prepare before they added themselves to her honor guard. All the Weres who'd been with her through the temple both times, a smattering of humans armed with guns and cojones, and a handful of other wolves who'd drifted in from other towns or regions to join up or relieve the current patrols met up with her.

To be safe, she let Sheriff Browne and his deputies stay behind, along with eight Weres who guarded the town from either side in two groups of four. No one thought that the Venatori would bother with Greenhearth again, not when their deity had the chance to kill Bailey herself.

The werewitch ended her rounds at her house. Her brothers were sitting on the porch, waiting for her.

"Hey!" Kurt shouted. "You assholes need a permit to bring a parade out here. This is private property!"

Jacob threw an empty plastic coleslaw dish at his brother's head. Then he turned to the crowd. "If you need us," he stated, "we're here."

Bailey sighed and shook her head. "You guys are legal adults. I can't tell you you're not allowed to come. If you do, you're under my command, so if I tell you to duck, you better fuckin' well *duck*."

Russell pointed out, "You're the oldest. You make the plays, we back them."

A lump formed in the girl's throat, and she swallowed it and coughed. "All right. Come along then, dipshits. We got to meet back up with the government guys. Amazingly, they showed up early."

Soon the army filled the town square. Before Bailey and Velasquez could confer, Fenris stepped into the center of the crowd from nowhere, as usual.

"All of you know who I am," he proclaimed, "and if you don't, you will soon. I must remind you of a very important fact: *I cannot fight this battle for you.* There are ancient and ironclad rules against it, despite our adversary breaking those rules. I *can* support and advise, but that is all. This fight must be won by mortals, whether werewolf, witch, or human."

Velasquez smiled in a grim way. "We're prepared to win."

Bailey raised a hand. "We'll go over tactics in more detail after we portal, but for now, the idea is that we're going to head into the Other, then I'm going to telepathically contact the goddess and summon her. Challenge her, in a nutshell. From what Agent Velasquez has said, she's likely to take the bait. All of you guys will hide until the time is right. Then I'll need her lackeys off my back while I link to her and ground her magic, like with a lightning rod, draining her of power until she's dead or until I can throw it back at her."

Charlene quipped, "This ought to be something, all right. I thought I was good at magic, but…"

Fenris stepped closer to Bailey and spoke softly into her ear.

"I can help after a fashion, bending the rules but not breaking them outright. Rather than directly intervene, you can use me as a magical anchor to steady yourself while you siphon off Aradia's energy. *I* won't be acting or casting spells. It will simply be you drawing upon my reservoir of strength."

She put a hand on his arm. "Okay. Thank you for the umpteenth time for all you've done for us."

Turning to the crowd, Bailey announced, "Time to go."

Fenris raised his arms, chanting, then made a motion like tearing open both doors of a wardrobe. A glowing gate appeared before him, wide enough for three men abreast, and gasps went around the square.

Bailey turned to Velasquez. "This'll be you gentlemen's first time off Planet Earth, won't it?"

"Affirmative," the agent responded and ran a finger under his collar. "Ought to be interesting. Let's do it."

Bailey went first, and over a hundred people from three species followed her.

They emerged onto a flat, swampy plain surrounded by hillocks covered with gnarled black trees, and slate-colored clouds filled a dark-indigo sky. Mist curled from the boggy ground. The area looked familiar, but Bailey didn't know if she'd been here before since many places in the arcane realm were hard to distinguish from others.

Roland swept an arm before him as he stepped to the side. "Welcome to the Other! It's the universe's dumping ground for magical residue. Pretty cool, right?"

Something howled eerily in the distance.

Jacob blinked. "You guys have been spending all your time in here? I figured it was...nice, maybe. This is like a fucked-up version of Dagobah."

The werewitch shrugged. "You get used to it after a while. Oh, if anyone sees any wraiths or mist demons, just say so, and we'll blast the shit out of them. They don't usually come around Roland or me anymore, though."

Once everyone was through and had recovered from the initial disorientation, Bailey, Fenris, and Velasquez started choosing their setup for the battle to come. Everyone agreed that Bailey should wait on the plain, with her allies hidden in the dense, shadowy forests surrounding it.

"Shifters, off to that side," the werewitch said and gestured. "Fenris, are you allowed to wrangle them before the battle starts?"

"Yes," he confirmed. "I can at least get everyone ready and work on building pack-consciousness prior to Aradia's appearance."

Bailey nodded. "Good. Casters, off to that side. Don't be straight across from the Weres since we don't want to catch each other in a crossfire. Roland and Dante, you guys will be in charge of your species there. Can you work on cloaking us? Except me, obviously."

"Sure," Dante commented. "It'll take a minute, but we've got a ton of witches, so it ought to be a powerful enough illusion to fool a goddess. Hopefully."

Roland added, "She'll probably scan for your aura before she comes through, and if we can mask our auras, she might not check too hard before she shows up. No illusion is impervious, though, so we kinda have to pray she screws up."

Bailey told them to do it, and hoped for the best.

Velasquez said, "I'll take my men to the other side of the plain. Our weapons have plenty of range. We'll position ourselves so we form a triangle around them, and will be unlikely to hit the other two forces as long as everyone sticks to their assigned sector."

"Sounds good," Bailey confirmed. "Take up your positions, then. We'll be doing this soon. First, I need to talk to my damn teacher for a minute, and," she sucked in a deep breath, "think. Meditate."

As the agents, witches, and lycanthropes melted into their parts of the surrounding forest, Fenris remained by Bailey's side.

He urged, "Remember everything that I have taught you. You will need all of it. But if any mortal being can do this, it's you. You have my faith, Bailey. And when you're ready, we will help you."

They went over the protocol for both summoning and destroying the Order's divine patron. Once it was fresh in Bailey's mind, the wolf-god took his leave and disappeared into the woods to organize the Weres. The witches then wove their cloaking spell over all three of the auxiliary forces.

Bailey sat alone on the damp plain, mist and total silence around her. She breathed in and out, calming her mind while steeling her will and courage.

There is no other way to approach this, she told herself, *than to go straight through the middle. And the time has come.*

Although her friends and allies were all around, she realized she'd never felt more alone in her life.

CHAPTER FOURTEEN

The werewitch concentrated. As she'd done while conjuring her aura-clones, she focused on the manifestation of her power, condensing it into a projection of her image, consciousness, and personality, then sought the one she meant to draw out.

She imagined her astral body traveling through the veil between dimensions, across vast stretches of land and water, and descending upon Lyon, France, homing in on the greatest source of magical power in the region, if not all of Europe. One particular representative of the arcane stood out like a purplish-black flame amidst the gray void of the astral plane.

Aradia!

As her body reposed cross-legged on a boggy heath in the Other, Bailey saw a great stone hall before her, although it was indistinct, as if viewed through a churning tinted liquid or a video screen distorted by static.

Vaguely she made out a ring of women, all of them

talented sorceresses, and above and behind them another figure that was humanoid but not mortal. It gave the impression of both a beautiful lady and dark figure of deep menace, and it roiled in tones of black and gold and burgundy-violet.

Bailey Nordin, the goddess addressed her. The voice was oddly calm and hushed but resonant with malignant potency.

Hey! the girl replied. *'Sup? I heard you were looking for me. Must've been tough since I had to come find you.*

Faint murmurings came from the Venatori elders, but the goddess ignored them. She gave the impression of sneering at the werewitch.

How dare you address me thus? Aradia snapped. *Calling me up the way you'd summon a familiar and behaving like a spoiled child.*

Bailey channeled all the contempt and mockery she was capable of into her response.

Kiss my ass. Or if you're not up for that, turn around, bend over and show me yours, so I can either spank it or kick it—your choice. I dunno which you'd prefer, but you seem like the type of kinky little shit who'd be into getting paddled.

A thunderous ripple went through the astral murk. Bailey must have struck a nerve.

You will pay, the goddess raged, her voice seeming louder and less composed, *for addressing me in front of my finest witches like that. You are not only a mortal but a lycanthrope, a beast that plays at being human. I will reduce you to far less than that. Slowly.*

Okay, Bailey shot back. *Come and get me. Here's where I am.*

She flashed an image of herself sitting alone in a small, desolate valley within the Other.

I killed all your Inquisitors, the werewitch continued, *so you don't have anything else to throw at me, do you? Might as well fuck off, then, unless you want to send more witches to die. That's what deities do, isn't it? Sacrifice mortals like worthless chess pawns? It's what you've been doing all this time.*

Bailey felt a wave of uncertainty go through the hall. The senior Venatori recognized that she had a point. Now Aradia was backed into a corner, risking the loyalty of the followers she'd cultivated.

I will come, the goddess stated with icy matter-of-fact-ness, *and deal with you myself.*

The werewitch visualized her astral body making a Bruce-Lee-style come-on gesture, then spinning around and sticking out her ass.

Pucker up to plant a nice big kiss on it, and bring a damn ice pack for your own while you're at it because I'm gonna shove my boot so far up the thing that your colon will be feeling my—

Bailey jerked in place, falling over onto the moist peaty ground and blinking as she trembled. It took a moment for her to orient herself. Aradia had ended the transmission by destroying the girl's astral projection, cutting off communication.

She rose to her feet, inhaling and recharging her aura with residual magic from the Other.

"Must've worked," she muttered. "I bet she isn't wasting any time, either."

Recalling that time passed differently in the Other, the girl realized that two hours' preparation back on Earth might, in here, seem like two seconds.

And so it did.

The air about five hundred feet across the small plain ripped and an entire column of figures sprang out, fifty or more, filling the space before the portal. At their head was their divine patron.

Aradia in person gave off much the same impression Bailey had received during the arcane transmission, although the details were clearer—a tall woman of aristocratic beauty, with well-coiffed black hair, dressed in sable robes that curled and wafted about her as if she were underwater. Gold jewelry adorned her at every conceivable point, and her eyes flashed with darkly intense fire. She floated five or six feet above the ground.

Of the witches she'd brought with her, none were dressed in the black leather of Inquisitors. They all seemed to be regular troops.

All save four.

At the corners of the formation were figures unlike any Bailey had seen. They were completely concealed by strange outfits that looked like hooded robes made of leather scales reinforced with charcoal-hued armor. Glossy black masks covered their faces. Bailey suspected one of them was male, but the other three were clearly female. Each held a different weapon from disparate periods of history. There was no way to tell which were still living and which were technically dead. They were the Dread-knights, Aradia's most fearsome servants.

Bailey cleared her throat. On a deep level, she was terrified, but it wasn't her nature to let it show.

"What's this shit?" she inquired. "I thought you were

gonna come by yourself, not backed up by all your wussy little girlfriends."

An unpleasant yet familiar voice rang out of the crowd as a witch whom Bailey recognized pushed her way to the front of the formation.

"Wussy? Hah!" Madame MacLachlan scoffed. "We're not the ones who bring half a town to attack two women. Oh wait, that was your poof of a boyfriend. He must have mistaken you for a man. You're hardly in the position to boast anyway. May I kill this little numpty myself, Mistress? It'll be dead easy unless she's got her friends hiding around somewhere, which is possible. Either way, we'll be back home in no time."

Aradia ignored her. "It is a waste of my time, Bailey," she said, "to crush an insect such as you. I am merely here to oversee the inevitable. My daughters can deal with you with only cursory support from me."

The werewitch shuddered inwardly. Aradia's in-person voice was subtly horrible to the ear. It sounded like a person whispering from underwater into a megaphone that had been cranked up to unnatural volume.

"Oh, gosh," Bailey retorted. "Well, then. Wish I'd brought some backup of my own."

MacLachlan, who for all her obnoxiousness was not an idiot, recoiled as if slapped, but Aradia seemed to have difficulty with human sarcasm. The goddess grinned with hideous arrogance.

"Wait," the girl added, "I did. *Get her!*"

The curtain of the illusion fell away, and the black woods around them came alive with dozens of swarming figures. Weres shifted into quadrupedal form and bounded out from behind Bailey's right shoulder. Witches formed up behind her left, arms twisting with spells already being cast. Across the small valley, a man in a dark suit and glasses led his fatigue-wearing followers in firing blasts of magenta plasma at the Venatori's flanks.

Bailey shielded and then fell back three steps, knowing she'd have to seize control of the situation soon. For the moment, it was in their interest to let total chaos engulf the plain.

Leather-clad sorceresses shrieked and cursed as they struggled to adjust their formation. They were disciplined enough that it took only a second or two, but that was enough time for a couple of them to take wounds and others to be knocked around in the confusion.

Plasma beams ricocheted off hastily-thrown-up shields and burned holes through giant black trees. A witch screamed as two wolves pulled her out from amidst her comrades to rip her to shreds. Another wolf yelped in pain as lightning struck him and flung him to the ground. The casters of the Pacific Northwest collaborated on strange spells to create even more disorder while also defending their allies.

Amidst the melee, Aradia drifted upward, back, and down toward the portal she'd opened. Bailey feared the goddess was going to retreat, but instead, she absorbed the portal into herself and dispersed its energy. She was forcing her underlings to fight to the death while waiting until the last possible moment to engage in divine intervention.

She feared the consequences of breaking the rules,

Bailey grasped. But it seemed likely that Aradia *would* move to destroy her if it looked as though the Venatori would lose the battle.

The outcome was by no means certain.

Bailey hung back, saving her strength for her duel with the goddess but directing her followers as best she could and protecting them from attacks. "Neutralize that!" she ordered a cluster of witches. "You guys!" she shouted to a couple of Weres, "distract her!" In between issuing commands, she swatted magical attacks out of the air and bolstered her force's morale with positive psionic messages.

Everything that had happened thus far had taken what would have been seconds in Earth-time. Bailey's army had greater numbers and the advantage of surprise, but the Venatori rallied swiftly, and then the advantage shifted.

The Dreadknights, who had done nothing in the first moments of violence, moved in unison. All four swung their archaic weapons, and a ringing flash like the breaking of a thunderstorm split the air. Dozens of Weres and witches hurtled up and away from the Venatori, flung like toys by the detonation of pure kinetic-magical force.

Bailey's eyes bulged. The Dreadknights had not been able to concentrate their power into killing blows, but the raw strength of their counterattack, not to mention their coordination, meant that the four of them alone might be a match for her entire group.

They needed to shift tactics and fast.

The werewitch sent out a telepathic message to her Weres, to whom she was the most strongly connected, commanding them to apply hit-and-run methods rather than direct force. They circled, moving more than they attacked, nipping and hamstringing, drawing attention or simply bowling Venatori troops aside when they saw an opening.

At the same time, she shouted for her witches to pin down the Order's sorceresses while directly attacking the magical essence that powered the Dreadknights. This wasn't enough to stop the four elites from attacking, but it disrupted their unity and meant they had less support from the regulars.

Velasquez, grasping what Bailey was trying to do, had his men move and fire, move and fire in alternating patterns in a continual suppressive barrage that vaporized a handful of the weaker Venatori and even did slight damage to one of the Dreadknights.

The quartet of deadly mage-warriors was far from defeated. With shocking abruptness, they carved through swathes of Bailey's allies, conjuring hurricanes of fire, tidal waves of electrified acid, hailstorms of jagged steel, and earthquakes of ice and mist. Bailey tried to shield her people from the worst of it, but at least a dozen were struck down, and she knew at least half of them were dead.

Madame MacLachlan, cackling madly, uprooted a cluster of trees and deprived the Weres of their closest hiding places, then started tossing the huge trunks toward the wolves. Bailey shot down most of them with lightning and threw one tree back at the witch. She squealed in irritation and fell back behind her subordinates, vanishing from sight amidst the raging struggle.

The battle dragged on, neither side gaining the upper hand. Both forces saw their numbers dwindle and their strength sag, and both fought on with crazed desperation. The casualty rate had climbed to a quarter of both contingents.

This can't go on, Bailey grated. *Why won't Aradia fight me? I can almost see an opening to get to her...*

A bolt of plasma the size of a redwood streaked past her ear and she barely shielded herself from being burned by its convective heat, pushing the blast into the swamp and away from her friends.

Then the girl locked eyes with the goddess. Her insides threatened to liquefy as a terrible fact made itself clear: Aradia could obliterate her in an instant. The deity was choosing not to, not yet, holding onto the hope that her servants could do the job for her and eliminate the possibility of retaliation from the rest of the divine realm.

It also appeared that Aradia was controlling the Dreadknights through brute force of will, which would explain the elite troops' robotic unanimity.

Fuck. She's smarter than I thought. I've got to engage her now. Without me directing the fight, our guys won't have the coordination or morale I could give them, but if I don't take out Aradia, we're screwed anyway.

Bailey focused on the Dreadknight closest to her, who had positioned herself between the werewitch and the goddess. A two-handed iron mace was gripped in the gauntleted hands, and sudden slashes of the weapon sent brutal sonic shockwaves toward Aradia's enemies.

Extending her hand out flat, Bailey summoned a plasma blade on the mace's haft. It split asunder with a sound like a massive gong and the Dreadknight staggered back, stumbling out of the straight line she'd occupied between her mistress and her foe.

The way was open. Bailey reached out toward Aradia and prepared to finish the job—if the witch-goddess didn't finish her first.

CHAPTER FIFTEEN

*F*enris, Bailey beseeched, *Father of all Weres. Please, please tell me you're still here. Please tell me you knew what you were talking about. Please help me in any way you can. Fenris!*

In the back of her mind, it struck her that she was *praying*. Fenris was, after all, her god.

She perceived his presence, oddly cold and grim yet comforting with his wisdom and strength. She'd locked onto Aradia, and the goddess might have realized that the wolf-deity was present or that Bailey was calling out to him. If so, she probably thought Bailey was merely crying in desperation.

She was wrong.

Silently, the werewitch chanted the intonation her mentor had taught her, anchoring herself to Fenris like an appliance is plugged into an electrical socket. No conscious thought emanated from him. In observance of the rules, he had remained wholly passive throughout the battle, yet she sensed enormous power, a reservoir that, compared to her own, was nearly bottomless.

Then she grounded herself in the dismal enchanted substance of the Other, setting her body up to act as a conduit through which excess arcane energy could be channeled before being bled out into the basic stuff of the dimension. By its very nature, the Other absorbed magic the way a sponge soaked up water.

Finally, the werewitch imagined a grasping, luminous cord or vine or tentacle extending from her forehead to plug into the heart of the deity who had founded the Venatori Order and caused so much suffering.

The conduit was established. Bailey gasped.

So did Aradia, visibly and audibly, resembling a human for a brief instant. The goddess' half-lidded eyes flew open, blazing with alarm. Bailey *felt* her fear as she realized what the werewitch was about to do.

The first moment of connection between the two beings was like an explosion in Bailey's mind. As with her locking into Fenris as a backup anchor, there was a sense of overwhelming might and unfathomably deep wells of arcane power. But in all other respects it was different, due both to the nature of the connection and the personality of the goddess.

In contrast to the cool stolidity of the wolf-deity, Aradia's mind blazed with anger, supercilious loathing, and an alien self-righteousness that had no interest in understanding mortals' point of view.

Overlaying these emotions was a sharp shriek of abject terror, so awful in its intensity that Bailey almost felt pity for the goddess. The threat of annihilation was bad enough for creatures destined to die. It was many times worse for an entity for whom immortality was the norm.

Yet Bailey did not back off. Aradia had come here to kill her and all her people, family and friends, alongside her. The werewitch would do whatever it took to stop her.

The goddess felt *that*, too.

"Destroy her!" Aradia screamed, her bizarre voice more hideous than ever with its edge of panic. "Stop the werewitch! Kill her!"

In accordance with the witch queen's will, her bound servants jumped as though they'd been jabbed with cattle prods. They flung themself toward Bailey, their intent to kill her now double its former strength.

The wolves and witches of the Northwest interposed themselves and their powers, however, and the agents of the United States government fired their plasma guns with deadly accuracy. Again there was a general clash of violence against violence, but neither side gained the advantage.

The battle reached a lull as the grounding process began. Bailey drew raw power through the channel she had opened.

Everyone stared in shock as a blinding light, both terrible and magnificent, emanated from the goddess' form. It was so intense as to be impossible to look at near the edge of her physical shape, yet it wavered and lessened as it moved away from her, like flames or like a liquid spraying from a pressurized source. It was power, pure magical essence, and it was being bled out of her.

Aradia, her eyes wrathful, snapped a gold-bedecked arm toward a group of four Weres clustered at her right flank. Bailey watched in horror as the shifters were engulfed in the shining white blaze, burning through them in a flash and reducing them to mounds of pale, bleached dust. It had happened too fast for her to do anything, especially with ninety-nine percent of her attention focused on grounding and destroying the goddess.

But her observation about Aradia's power fading as it leaked out of her proved accurate. The white flames were incredibly bright, but they dissipated into nothingness mere yards from the spot where the quartet of werewolves had perished. One other wolf stumbled back, howling in fear and pain, but he had only superficial burns to fur and skin and rolling on the damp ground extinguished the heat easily enough.

Too much of the deity's power, vast though it was, had been siphoned away from her.

Blobs of light with tails of radiant flame emerged from Aradia like comets and spiraled toward Bailey. Most of them streaked past her or swirled around her briefly and then sunk into the ground, which absorbed them with glowing flickers that resembled lightning within an approaching thunderhead.

But some of the spectral fireballs flowed into Bailey. She felt energized and invigorated but also jittery and shocked. She hadn't expected that to happen, and she didn't know how to deal with it.

"Back!" she shouted to her allies. "Fight them, but everyone get back from Aradia!"

And me, she thought but didn't say aloud.

The Dreadknights began to coordinate their efforts toward destroying the werewitch. Two of them threw crude but powerful waves of magic at their nemeses, knocking Weres back and pressing witches down in the desperate need to defend their goddess. With the cover this provided, the other two knights focused on Bailey.

For all that she'd been through, and all the courage she'd shown, the werewitch had to fight not to succumb to total panic. Victory hung by a thread. Everything depended on the next moment or two, and as the dark-armored elite warriors moved in with murderous purpose, she saw her death approaching—and with it, the failure of everything they'd strived for.

No, Bailey, not this fucking time or any other time, she urged herself. *We might want to fall to pieces since this goes beyond anything a mortal is supposed to deal with, but we're not doing it that way. We're winning this. Period.*

Amidst the chaotic violence, Bailey found herself strained by a kind of four-way tug-of-war as her attention, strength, will, and essence were acted upon from four different directions.

First there was the influence of Fenris, passive though it was, representing a massive reserve of strength and wisdom and arcane potency. Being connected to it, she felt a modicum of security, but being certain of how much or how little to draw upon was nearly impossible with everything else going on.

Second was the continual hemorrhage of power from Aradia, flowing toward and through her into the Other's magically created earth, some of it seeming to lodge in Bailey's being as it passed, while the rest dissolved into the substance of the bog.

Third was the reaction from the goddess—the interplay

of Aradia trying to pull her immortal life force back into her, and at other times, hurling it out and around her in a crazed effort to destroy her enemies.

Fourth and finally, Bailey's mind was on the verge of tearing itself asunder. She didn't know if she was doing things right, she didn't know if she would succeed, she didn't know if any of her friends would survive. There was nothing she could do but forge ahead with the insanity of desperation and hope it worked out.

And still the battle raged.

Madame MacLachlan had begun using telekinesis to lift the two Dreadknights who were fighting Bailey's allies, tossing them from position to position, the better for them to quickly unleash devastating attacks on any group of Weres or witches who got too close.

"Ha-ha! None of you numpties can overcome the simplest tactic imaginable. You'll all be carbon paste in no time!"

Roland, who was trying to fend off a surge of acid rain while his friends attacked the Dreadknights, had to admit the Scotswoman had a point.

"Okay, then," he murmured, and reached out with his telekinetic hand, grabbing the nearest Dreadknight, the male, and hurling him toward MacLachlan. The armored witch collided with Madame and both hit the ground. The brief reprieve allowed Jon, Trevor, and Charlene to take out a regular Venatori caster with a hasty combined-arms strike.

Meanwhile, Velasquez and three of his men managed to cut through the cluster of arcane shields to hit one of the Dreadknights moving toward Bailey with their plasma beams. The projectiles couldn't defeat the knight through its heavy enchanted armor, but they slowed it down and forced it to respond by casting a spell to deflect the arcanoplasm back. The agents scattered as random pulses of magenta-white fire rained down around them. One man took a terrible burn to the chest and arm and had to be pulled away from the front line.

Bailey mentally stabilized the core of her being. The forces tugging on her would continue doing their own thing for now. She had to focus on the second thing—draining Aradia of her power.

Watching her people suffer and die in the heat of combat only strengthened her resolve.

I can do this, she thought. *It's like opening a fire hydrant, is all. Shit, didn't Fenris say when he was first training me to use magic that that was what I shouldn't be like? A spraying pipe? Well, it's different this time. There's only so much water, and we're gonna keep draining it until Aradia is done for.*

As the stress and strain increased, so did Bailey's ability to deal with it. Not only because she was starting to understand what she was doing, but because more and more of the arcane flow from the goddess was streaming into her. The majority was entering her body and empowering her. Only a trickle shot past to vanish into the misty ground.

Bailey was *taking* the goddess' power.

"*No!*" Aradia raged, every last semblance of composure gone from her as she entered a new spasm of fury.

Her limbs flailed, her eyes bulged, and her hair came loose to waft about her head like a mass of black tentacles. Hissing as she sucked in breath, the witch-deity then expelled it in an outward strike with both hands, employing the strength that remained to her in a final act of divine destruction.

A ripple of mostly invisible sonic-concussive force shot out from Aradia in a circular shockwave and tailing it was a moving wall of blue-white fire. Bailey tried to redirect some of her newfound stolen magic to stop it, but the intense concentration of the grounding process interfered. She was too slow.

Everyone except the werewitch was bowled over. The goddess' friends and foes alike toppled and crashed to the ground as the shockwave hit them. And then the people closest to her, including most of the remaining Venatori as well as twenty or so Weres and local witches, were blasted with the bright flames.

Bailey swallowed her horror as half the bodies caught in the firestorm were burned to death in seconds. The others were merely scorched and discombobulated and sent rolling across the plain toward the surrounding woods.

She could feel the fear the attack had created. The surviving Venatori felt their mistress had gone mad and forsaken them, and Bailey's forces had started to believe they were fighting an opponent who could not be defeated.

But Bailey knew better. Aradia had exhausted herself, conjuring the mighty blast. She didn't have much vitality left.

"Dreadknights!" the deity shrieked. "Kill the werewitch *now*! Kill her lover, the traitor he-witch, and the pack alphas!"

Her knights had only been knocked off-balance by the attack; the flames had not harmed them through their armor. They resumed their prior strategy of having two of their number advance on Bailey while the other pair went after her friends.

But the elite mage-warriors drew their strength and took their direction straight from Aradia. Bailey, her mind conjuring an image of taking a massive gulp of air or water, siphoned a huge mass of arcane essence away. So much that it threatened to overwhelm her, but after a moment of dizziness, she held firm.

Aradia sank from the air to the ground. Her feet touched the earth, then she crumpled to her knees, squinting and balling her fists in fear, anger, and pain. The Dreadknights faltered, swaying on their feet as if drunk.

Bailey was so intent on the spectacle in front of her that it took a few heartbeats before she realized what had happened to her. She no longer stood in front of the goddess, separated by a short stretch of boggy heath, but floated in the air.

"Look!" a woman shouted. "Look at Bailey!"

The werewitch's feet dangled two yards above the earth. Motes of brilliant starlight swirled around her, blinking and shining from an iridescent cloud of pure magic, the overflow of the divine power that had once been Aradia's and was now hers. She closed her eyes and felt as if she were a sun with an entire solar system orbiting her body, and a rush went through her that was both chillingly cold and blazing hot.

When she opened her eyes, they shone furious crimson light like the eyes of her wolf-form, but far brighter and more striking. A hurricane of power spun within her.

Fenris started to cut her off from himself, slowly

retracting with a profound satisfaction that was faintly arrogant. He was proud of her, but there was more to it than that.

Bailey had no time to think about it, though. She opened her mouth and spoke.

"*It's over!*"

Her voice was clear and ethereal, like a peal of thunder and a chorus of trumpets all at once. It echoed over the plain and through the foggy woods and swamps that stretched for leagues in every direction. It shook everyone who heard it, then awed them into silence.

"It's over," Bailey repeated. "The balance has shifted, and the tide has turned. The power that used to be Aradia's is hers no longer. We have a new goddess, one born of both witches and Weres, who represents the best interests of both. That's *me*. I'm not bound by the laws and oaths made by the previous deities, and all of this insanity is done with *today*!"

Her glowing eyes saw the faces of the people before her. Those of her friends and the individuals who had rallied to her proverbial banner, who stared with stunned reverence and mounting relief. Those of the Venatori, flabbergasted and feeling helpless anger and frustration. And the face of Aradia, borderline pitiful but still malignant with loathing.

In the moment of silence that followed, Bailey thought of Fenris. He had not mentioned the possibility that Bailey could attain the power of a deity, but he *must* have known it could happen. He must have.

That left the question, had he neglected to mention it to spare her the extra worry and anxiety over the ramifications? Or was it perhaps something he'd hoped would happen all along?

But there was no time to ponder the matter. The Venatori were preparing to make a last stand, and they might kill more of Bailey's friends, even if they had no chance against the werewitch.

She didn't give them the chance.

Bailey shouted wordlessly and extended her arms, throwing out a crackling electrical storm cloud that covered the air above the plain. With no difficulty whatsoever, she manipulated the energies that churned within it, and powerful bolts of lightning descended upon the remaining Venatori regulars, cracking through their shields and striking them down with an overload of voltage. The other witches, the lycanthropes, and the agents backed away from the lethal spectacle.

The four Dreadknights charged her. She waved her hand and they screeched to a halt mid-stride as though they'd crashed into an invisible wall of thick foam, their arms flailing.

Bailey dealt with the first knight via a meteor of roaring black fire that struck her and engulfed both body and armor in supernatural heat, reducing the figure to ash in the blink of an eye.

"Holy shit!" one of the agents exclaimed.

Bailey encased the second knight in thick ice at absolute zero, then tossed an invisible lance of percussive force into the man's armored center and shattered him into hundreds of frosty shards.

The third struggled forward a step, hoisting a bronze Mycenaean-era sword over her head. Bailey opened a chasm under her feet and she toppled in. It closed around her, leaving only earth where she'd been.

The fourth, the one whose sex was unclear, waved a fist at Bailey in a final gesture of defiance. She responded by blinking at the figure. When her eyes opened, metal and flesh had turned to stone. Then she blew toward it the way one would puff out a candle flame, and under the enchanted wind that resulted, the statue crumbled to powdery dust.

"Curse you!" It was Aradia, still determined to fight back even as she slumped to the ground, looking wan and haggard and barely like a supernatural being anymore. The long-nailed hand rose and cast a bolt of arcanoplasm at Bailey's face.

She swept it aside as if it were a spitwad, and it streaked into the sky and was gone.

Bailey's eyes glowed still brighter. "Like I said, Aradia, it's over."

The werewitch swept her hands straight down. A column of white light and plasma that were too intense for mortals to look at descended from the heavens and engulfed the decrepit former goddess. Aradia's black silhouette was briefly visible within the ivory flame, then it dissolved into a cluster of shrinking black dots that quickly faded to nothing. As the rocket-like cacophony of the plasma strike ended, all that remained of the Venatori's deity was the faint echo of a wrathful, anguished scream.

Bailey floated back to the ground, her feet touching the dirt and weeds. The clearing was silent except for the usual sounds of the swamp. Of the people who still stood, and still lived, there were only her supporters, her partners, and her loved ones. Their enemies had been destroyed.

"We won," gasped Charlene, who crouched on the ground with an injured leg. "We actually frickin' *won!*"

Roland exhaled and fanned his face with a flapping hand. "Yeah, we did somehow. Hell. Nicely done, Bailey! That was kinda *scary* in all honesty, but it was certainly impressive."

The werewitch felt her powers receding. They weren't needed now, or at least there was no reason to be so theatrical with them. Her eyes returned to normal.

"I'm still me," she said in her normal voice, although she wondered if that were true.

Then something flashed pink, and Roland, demonstrating better reflexes than Bailey would have credited him with, pivoted aside to dodge the thrust of a plasma sword.

"Oh, shite," Madame MacLachlan cursed, then she ran.

Weres and witches started to stumble after her, but crashed into each other and got bottlenecked by the dense woods. Bailey waved for them to stand aside, and she stepped into the place the final witch had recently occupied.

The Scotswoman called over her shoulder, "You haven't crushed the Order! Merely a symbolic victory. We'll be back in half a tick!"

Reaching a spot she assumed was safe, MacLachlan shielded her back and opened a portal right in front of her.

Bailey could have thrown a projectile through the shield, but there was a chance, however slim, that the sorceress could have caught it, given her immense talent at telekinesis. The werewitch decided not to bother. Instead, she pointed her index finger at the Scotswoman, who was on the verge of stepping through her gateway.

MacLachlan exploded, her body bursting apart in a spray of crimson particles that the breeze caught and wafted off as a pinkish mist. Her portal winked out, leaving the few chunks that remained to be shadowed by the trees.

Roland smiled. "With a cherry on top," he quipped.

CHAPTER SIXTEEN

With the battle won, a generalized celebration erupted, and Bailey did nothing to stop it. Her friends had earned the right to go a little nuts.

People cheered and laughed. Strangers hugged one another as though they'd been best friends since kindergarten. Wolves howled and leaped in the air. A couple of young Seattle witches took the center of the field and did cartwheels over patches of scorched earth.

All the while, the werewitch-goddess tended to the wounded. She knew little of healing spells, but with her newfound powers and with the Other's strange rejuvenating ability speaking to her in subtle voices, she was able to conjure patches of softly-glowing ambrosia that eased pain and stabilized the conditions of the injured. They would be okay until they could get to a hospital back on Earth, anyway.

Given the ferocity of the struggle, though, several of their friends were beyond help.

Old Mr. Holmquist lay among the fallen, but he'd died

avenging his son and protecting the rest of his family and his people. Shari, the younger of the two witches they'd recruited with Dante's help in the frozen yogurt shop, had also perished. Bailey didn't know them well, but she mourned them all the same.

The worst news, though, was that Roger had died fighting one of the Dreadknights. When he'd joined Bailey for the trials in the temple, he had fought with reckless bravery, trying to atone for his pack having stood by while their neighbors were wiped out. Bailey supposed his penance was more than done, and the Silver Stars would need a new alpha. She hoped whoever took Roger's place was as brave as he had been, but more restrained. Packs benefited from consistent leadership.

Roland and her brothers had survived. She wasn't sure if she could have handled losing any of them.

As the initial festivities settled down, the survivors dealt with the dead.

"The Other," Alfred Warner began, "is sacred, even the parts beyond the traditional holy ground of the Weres. Thus we should bury our dead here, in the place they gave their lives."

No one voiced any serious objections, so the lycanthropes took to digging graves for their lost brethren.

At the same time, the witches considered what to do. Deanna, Shari's friend, offered a suggestion. "Those who were consumed here should remain, but those who left intact bodies, we might as well take them back home."

Agreeing, the casters gathered their dead. The agents did likewise, some of them coming over to help their allies with the somber task. Agent Velasquez approached Bailey and Roland and Dante, surveying the scene.

Velasquez composed himself before he spoke. "It's tragic," he said, "that we lost as many people as we did here today. All of us."

Bailey and the others, including humans, witches, and Weres, nodded with solemn faces.

"But," the agent went on, "we all know what would have happened if we hadn't shown up to fight the good fight. Sometimes these kinds of sacrifices are justified. Uncle Sam knows it and appreciates it, and so will our kids and grandkids.

"And I have news. Townsend will live. I think he wanted to join Spall, but he's gonna have to wait. We need him."

The werewitch reached out and took his hand. "He'll be proud that we pulled it off. Spall would be, too."

Velasquez removed his glasses and looked into the distance. "Maybe one day we'll find out about that. Oh, and perhaps you can bring Townsend here and heal him all the way. But that can wait. We have a victory to celebrate."

Roland raised a hand. "We won the war for them. The witches and Weres of America united to take down the Venatori's goddess, and it's hard to see a cult of their sort recover from a blow like that anytime soon. If ever."

"They still have their headquarters in Lyon," Velasquez pointed out. "And their senior council sat the fighting out, so they still exist. But...we inflicted a hell of a lot of damage on them. We haven't been able to get the prisoners to say how many total members they have yet. It's possible that the lower-level witches aren't privy to that information. But there can't be *that* many of them, and given the number we've killed since this whole mess started, well, it's safe to say that they'll be having a personnel crisis for a while. Not to mention, they threw the biggest gun they had at us—their deity—and it failed. Ought to give them lots to ponder."

"No shit," Will Waldsbach agreed.

Dante asked Bailey, "Do you think we should continue the war? Go after them and finish them off? It might be the smart thing to do, but then again, it's unlikely they can *do* anything more to us at this point."

Bailey considered the prospect. With her newfound might, she could do it. The potential of them being able to threaten her or hers would be eliminated. But...

"No," she stated, "I don't think so unless they force my hand. We'll be on the lookout for a time yet, but if they're stupid enough to try something else after *today*, they're pretty much a shoo-in for a Darwin Award. No, I'm gonna say it's enough to send them up to their room without supper and let them think about what they've done."

The wizard and the agent gave slow nods.

"Yes," said Roland, "exterminating them might look bad to witchdom, even if they have it coming."

"And," added Velasquez, "keeping them around ought to help maintain a balance of power among the supernatural community in Europe. Another group of witches might challenge them for supremacy, and the Venatori will be busy trying to defend their position in their weakened state. With all that fuckery going on over there, *we* won't have to deal with them."

Dante laughed at that. "Spoken like a true representative of the US government. Still, you're right. There's no reason for us to risk overreaching ourselves. We've won. There's no other way to put it."

Roland turned to the other wizard. "You can be in charge of leading the rest of the Seattleites back home. I'll be staying with Bailey, naturally."

"Sounds good." Dante looked at his friends, particularly Charlene, who'd been watching him.

At that moment, footsteps approached, and the bystanders parted. Fenris strode into the little valley from the surrounding dark forest.

"Well done, everyone," said the wolf-god, his mouth rising a tad at the corners. "I've been listening, and you said most of what needed to be said. I don't have much to add besides my thanks and congratulations."

Wolves bowed their heads to him. Bailey approached and put her arms around his neck.

"Fenris, Marcus, or whatever," she told him, "thank you so damn much. Part of me can't believe we pulled this off, but the other part figured we were destined to or whatever. Maybe it's a mortal thing, kinda hard to explain."

Then she remembered that she might not *be* a mortal anymore.

As though reading her thoughts, Fenris commented, "We should talk alone for a short while."

She nodded. "Yeah. I was thinking the same thing."

The wolf-deity turned to the crowd and announced, "I will open portals for everyone to return home after I'm done speaking to Bailey."

The two of them went off into the woods, finding a small glade where a beam of purplish light fell from the sky to illuminate the space between the trees. Before Bailey could ask questions, Fenris began.

"As you might have suspected, you are effectively a goddess now," he proclaimed. "I knew it might happen, and in fact, it was my hope that it would."

Her mouth opened, but no words came out. She had no idea how to respond to what he'd told her.

"It is a way of helping you," the shaman-deity continued, "and also helping myself. The old laws and covenants keep me locked behind too many walls to give our people the help they need. You, as a newly-arisen divine being, are not bound by those."

It makes sense, she admitted to herself, *but still, I wish he'd have warned me. Might be the craziest thing that's happened so far, which is saying something.*

Fenris took a step forward and laid a hand on her shoulder. "Well done. Later, I will begin training you—again—to deal with your new powers. But for now, go home and take a much-deserved rest."

"Yeah," she agreed, "I do deserve a rest, don't I? Roland too."

Together, they walked back to the plain to begin opening the portals that would carry the victorious back to their homes.

Bailey and Roland slept. They shared her bed in her room at the old farmhouse in the northwest corner of Greenhearth. Exhausted as they were, sleeping was all they'd done so far.

That was fine with both of them. They slumbered deeply and well, languorous and relaxed, in the patch of soft warmth they'd made next to each other. No one bothered them. They didn't have to be up at any particular time.

Bailey woke up and stayed up before Roland did. Her clock read 11:36. Once she came to and decided she'd slept enough, she sat up straight, rubbed her eyes, and looked at her lover. His mouth was hanging open. Kinda undignified, but otherwise, his aristocratically handsome face was placid, his light hair tousled in a way that flattered him.

She thought about waking him but figured he could use the extra rest. She dressed and went downstairs.

Her brothers had gone off somewhere, although the coffee pot was still on and had about three cups' worth left in it. Judging by its thick, intense blackness, it had to be Russell's. Bailey poured a mug. It woke her up damn quick.

Jacob had left her a note.

Bailey, we needed to spend quality guy-time with the Weres who lost friends or brothers. You know that we're still here for you and can be back in two seconds if you need us. Take care.

Later, she'd have to spend quality sibling time with *them.*

After a shower, she pulled on her boots and walked into town. She could have easily driven, but she felt like walking. Getting to the diner wouldn't take very long, and it was a beautiful day, even if the sky was partly covered by clouds. It looked like it had rained last night.

Two-thirds of the way to the Elk, as Bailey took a turn toward the establishment, a group of four teenagers caught her attention.

A girl of maybe fifteen was being hassled by three boys

who were around the same age, perhaps a year or two older. From what Bailey overheard, the boys were throwing their proverbial weight around, threatening the girl with their family connections and trying to impress her with their achievements since she'd apparently brushed them off earlier.

"Listen," urged one of the guys, "you have to be married off within a few years, and you're not gonna find anyone better than us unless you want to marry some old fuck. You're wasting time."

"I already told you," the girl snapped back, although there was a note of fear in her voice, "to let me go and stop following me around. Okay?"

Bailey stepped in. "Excuse me. Is there a problem?"

All four pairs of eyes snapped toward her.

"Oh," the boy who'd spoken a moment ago began, "uh, no. You're Bailey, aren't you?" He and his friends fidgeted uncomfortably.

The girl growled, "They won't leave me alone."

The werewitch pursed her lips and regarded the group with a steady gaze. "Sounds pretty cut and dried. You boys run along. Leave her alone."

She could see the emotions clashing in the boys' brains: their fear of her, combined with their unwillingness to *seem* afraid or to abandon the chase. The leader of the young men hit her with a question she wasn't expecting.

"You gonna blow us into burnt pieces or something if we don't?" He grunted. It wasn't a challenge, exactly. He was informing her that for all her power, she couldn't get away with murdering teenagers on the streets of her own town.

Bailey crossed her arms over her chest. With the new power she'd attained, she could have done pretty much anything she wanted to them: lifted them into the air, floated them over the mountains and out of the Hearth Valley, or told them via psionics to walk their asses home. But most of the town didn't know what to make of her as a werewitch. What would they think if everyone knew she was a goddess?

Instead, she told the boys, "No. However, if you don't stop harassing this girl, I'll *stop* you from doing so. Got it?"

The leader chewed a lip. He stepped forward, jutting out his chin, and put an arm back over the girl's shoulder as if he were protecting her from Bailey, absurd though that was. His friends came up on the side. The smallest one, Bailey realized, was human, although the leader and the other one were lycanthropes.

"Listen," he insisted, "this is none of your business. Don't you have more important stuff to do? We–"

Bailey charged them.

It was over in half a minute. After all the exhaustive magical shit she'd done lately, she appreciated a little old-fashioned ass-kicking. She didn't hurt them too badly. None would need to go to the hospital. They were just dumb kids. She simply convinced them that their course of action was unwise, and they ought to reconsider it.

They did. The human fled, rubbing his bruised jaw, and a second later, the two Weres joined him, one hobbling from the moderate groin-kick he'd taken, and the other nursing a fat lip and bruised abdomen.

The girl sighed in relief. "Thank you, Bailey. They used to be my friends, but they've been acting weird lately. I think it's because we're getting older, so now everyone is talking about this marriage stuff."

Bailey looked at the young woman. She had auburn hair and a longer face, but otherwise, she might have been looking at herself nine or ten years ago.

"I understand," the werewitch stated. "Believe me. I was about to get some, uh, brunch, I guess, at the Elk. Want to join me? I'll pay."

"Okay." The girl smiled.

After they reached the diner and ordered their food, the young woman, whose name was Shelley, confided her fears about the future.

"It doesn't seem right," she muttered, "that we have to be married off by a certain age. I'm not even out of high school yet. What if I want to, I dunno, do something else?"

Bailey paused. "Shelley, I promise it won't happen. Things can change, and if I have anything to say about it, they will."

***

"Hey!" a familiar voice called. Bailey looked up.

It was Roland. He'd emerged from the depths of her bed and caught up with her when she was mere steps from the lot in front of Gunney's shop.

"Hey," she returned. "Nice timing. You missed brunch, though."

He shrugged. "I had a PBJ back at the house. Any news?"

"Mm, no," she considered. "Not particularly. Town's quiet and things are pretty normal, all things considered. I taught three punk-ass kids a lesson, but not hard enough for anyone to get in trouble or have to worry about medical bills."

The wizard scratched his nose and looked at the sky. "Your restraint is admirable. Since you could have done far worse to them, last I checked."

"Thanks." She aimed a gentle punch at his stomach, but he caught it. "You're getting stronger, you know, for not being a Were."

"Also thanks," he said. "Let's go talk to the old man."

They approached the repair bays, which were empty of vehicles. Gunney was taking inventory of his tools and supplies.

"I heard that," he barked as they approached, without looking at them. "*Old*, my ass. Almost a decade still before I can collect Social Security, in theory."

Roland shrugged. "Late middle-aged, then?"

Bailey put a hand on Gunney's shoulder. "Listen, whatever your age is, there's stuff I have to tell you. So far, I haven't told anyone else, not counting the people who were with me for the battle there, since they saw with their own eyes."

"I'll listen," he replied, his voice low and gravelly. They went out back by the scrapyard, and Bailey recounted everything. Including Fenris' confirmation of what she'd suspected.

The mechanic's jaw dropped as she spoke. He swayed and shook his head. When it was over, he had to wipe his eyes before he could respond.

"I'll be goddamned," he breathed. Then he laughed. "I helped raise a goddess. *That's* interesting. And I still get to boss her around in the shop. Plus, you're technically a customer since you've got one of my rides."

Bailey cracked up. She hadn't expected him to react like this, but now that he had, she couldn't imagine him saying anything else.

"True," she conceded.

"Oughta be good for business." He fished around in the pockets of his overalls and produced a key. "Look over there." He indicated where with a movement of his head.

The Model T awaited, its shiny red paint a beacon of hope.

"I figure someone has to give it a test drive. Since you've still barely broken in the Camaro, I ain't giving it to you, but we'll see about the future. Still, take 'er out on the town."

She hugged him. "Will do. And don't worry, it'll come back in pristine condition, aside from a little mud."

Bailey fetched the wizard from the bay and hooked her arm around his elbow, guiding him toward the car.

"Hmm," he mused, "another new vehicle. Not sure I'm enough of a connoisseur to appreciate the finer points of how it handles compared to the other ones, but I'll take what I can get."

She nodded. "Yes, you will. Hop in."

Firing up the engine and waving goodbye to Gunney, she piloted the Model T out of the lot and onto the main road, cruising one or two miles per hour above the speed limit. It was just enough to appreciate the ride without risking an uncomfortable chat with the sheriff. Soon they were out of town, and Bailey turned onto a side road that led to a scenic overlook in the hills.

Roland folded his hands behind his head as he gazed at the Hearth Valley, which looked sleepy and peaceful in the fading daylight.

"So, what now, your Divine Majesty?" he asked.

She leaned over and kissed him on the mouth. "We take a deep, long breath and watch the sun set over this beautiful little town. Everything else can wait."

You made it! Here we are at the end of book 6. Thank you so much for reading this far.

Again, let me first express my heartfelt wishes that you and yours have made it through 2020 so far unscathed, or only minorly scathed (is that a word?). I mean, it's been a week since the last author notes. People have been bitten by alligators, and there is an entire raft of hurricanes waiting in the wings to attack the South. What else will this year bring?

This week, Jo and I hopped into the Jeep and headed to Southern California to visit Grandma. You know, white hair, delicious food, open arms? I needed some of that! Friday's dinner was *rolladen* and *rotkraut*, which those of you of German extraction know means a bit of heaven on your plate, along with fluffy mashed potatoes. For the rest of you, get some! You won't be sorry.

As I rolled southward, the smoke from the Oregon, NoCal, and SoCal fires covered the skies in varying degrees. I am so sad for those who have lost their homes and for the landscape we are losing, although it has been said that the redwood trees will survive. Thank goodness for that! Everyone I had contact with was smiling (well, how can you tell with a mask on, but their eyes crinkled) and enthusiastic. It was a pleasure, everyone! Hope I see you on the way back.

Still down here in Fallbrook, California, not heading back until midweek. Have laptop, will travel! It's hot down here, though. It was 100 Saturday. Jo is enjoying her walks on the beach in Oceanside. Much barking at seagulls ensues. Much nicer temp today and for the next few. Almost cold on the beach at sunset. Almost.

I always thank my advance reader team and the proof-reader team, the ones who read my stories after they are edited. They help make this book (and every book) its best. Couldn't do it without you, folks! Much appreciated!

I hope you enjoyed Bailey's and Boland's further adventures. They will be back. And if you get a moment, drop me a review, please. Those are the lifeblood of any writer. We appreciate you!

Until next time,
Renée

I COULDN'T DO THIS WITHOUT YOU!

Thanks to my early readers, you rock!

Angel LaVey, Dave Hicks, Deb Mader, Debi Sateren, Diane L. Smith , Dorothy Lloyd , James Caplan, Jeff Goode, Kerry Mortimer, Veronica Stephan-Miller

The WereWitch Series
Bad Attitude (Book One)
A Bit Aggressive (Book Two)
Too Much Magic (Book Three)
Were War (Book Four)
Were Rages (Book Five)
God Ender (Book Six)

Coming Soon
God Trials (Book Seven)
The Troll Solution (Book Eight)

Callie Hart Series
Thin Ice (Book One)
Cold Blood (Book Two)
Feelings Run Deep (Book Three)